When Time Stood Still

Laura Adams

Contents

Previously

Forced into prostitution at the hands of a drug lord, Dani escapes and starts her life over in Thailand.

Life is simple, yet perfect. She lives in a small beach hut with her partner Luke and their dog Buddy. She believes that the past is behind them; until it comes knocking on the door.

Thailand

Dani stood on the veranda while waiting on Luke. She rubbed coconut scented sun-cream onto her body while listening to the waves lap over one another rhythmically.

'Morning, Rebecca. Morning, Luke,' our neighbour shouted, waving from his terrace that was two along from where we lived.

'Morning, Joe.' Luke and I said in unison.

I still had to remind myself that I was now called Rebecca because Luke often still called me Dani, as did Elanor and my mum. I went by both names depending on where we were and whether we were alone. It had caused a few raised eyebrows when Luke accidentally called me Dani in front of other people, and I could see the accusation in their eyes as they looked at each other awkwardly, invisible thought bubbles popping out of their heads. The thoughts of *'he's having an affair'* hanging in the air.

'Come on, Buddy, let's go.' I threw the ball along the beach and Buddy, our rescue dog, chased after it, tail wagging as he retrieved his prize and made his way back to me, looking very pleased with himself.

'Good boy,' I said, giving him a pat. We walk to the water's edge and I let the waves lap over my feet while Buddy cooled off in the water and swam around in circles.

I placed my hands on top of my swollen stomach and imagined meeting our newest addition to the family in roughly two weeks' time. We had decided against finding out the sex of the baby, preferring for our little miracle to enter the world as a surprise to us both. We had two names picked, Tesha for a girl, which means survivor, and Chadd for a boy, which means protector. Our own precious baby seemed too good to be true after everything that had happened, but in some bizarre way, Luke and I had bonded over our experiences and supported each other through it. There had been many times that I had wanted to walk away from Luke, and there would always be a reminder of what I had been through, a hidden entity that would pop up without warning and try to pull me down the dark corridor into the past. Prior to getting pregnant, I had been back to the rehab centre twice for a three-day mini stay, which gave me a confidence boost when I was feeling vulnerable – and I had not relapsed.

Elanor had been living with us for the past six months and she was just as excited as Luke and I about the impending arrival of our bub. My mum was coming to stay for a few weeks and she was arriving next week, just in case the little one made an early appearance.

We were renting a house in the Chonburi province, which was one hundred KM south-east of Bangkok and a twelve-hour drive from Mai Khao. Both Luke and I had been offered work as English teachers in a local school, hence the move away from Mai Khao. It was a big step moving to Pattaya, but I had felt ready for it and confident that it was the right decision. I stayed in touch with the staff at the Soi Dog Foundation and felt so privileged that we had both played a part in helping out there and also rescuing one of the dogs. Our beautiful Buddy.

On the day that my mum was due to arrive, I woke up to damp bed sheets. At first, I thought that I had wet myself and I lay there mortified wondering how I would explain that to Luke. As I stood up to try and sneak to the toilet, water trickled down my legs and an invisible vice gripped my stomach forcing me to bend over and gasp in shock. I was in labour.

I left Luke sleeping and quickly showered and then I sat on the veranda and drank a cup of raspberry tea, it supposedly helped the uterus work better during labour. I focused on my breathing and placed my hands on my stomach, aware that soon, I would be holding my baby in my arms. My mum was due to arrive at one pm and right now, it was five-forty-five am.

I went into Elanor's room and gently shook her on the shoulder.

'Elanor, wake up,' I whispered, quietly.

'What's wrong, Dani, I mean, Rebecca? I wish I could get used to calling you another name!' She said, exasperated.

'It's the baby. My waters have broken, so I need to go to the hospital soon. Can I leave it up to you to call my mum and let her know I won't be at the airport to meet her?'

'Of course, honey. How do you feel? Are you in much pain?' She asked as she hurriedly stepped out of bed and gathered her clothes.

'I'm okay at the minute. I'm going to get Luke up now. Will you come with me to the hospital? I'd really like you to be there.'

'Try stopping me.' She smiled. 'Give me ten minutes and I'll be ready to go.' She quickly hugged me.

I walked into the bedroom where Luke was already stirring. He looked at me and then at his watch.

'You're up early, babe.'

'Baby Carter is about to make an entrance into the world so you need to get dressed and then drive me to the hospital.'

Luke jumped out of bed as if he was on fire and he was clearly more panicked than I was. It would have been funny if I had not been preoccupied with contractions.

I grabbed my hospital bag and Luke raced to place it in the car and then came back to help me. By the time we arrived at the hospital, the contractions were coming roughly five minutes apart and they were lasting about thirty seconds.

While I'd felt calm and in control an hour and a half ago, I was now feeling anxious and thinking about pain relief.

I was shown to my suite and my midwife, Annah, was waiting in the room for me. We had met throughout my pregnancy, so I felt completely at ease with her. She was German but spoke amazing English, as well as Thai, and she had lived here for the past five years.

'Rebecca, how are you feeling? I see that the baby wants to make an appearance on the day your mum arrives.' She smiled. 'Come and lay on here so that I can attach the fetal monitor and see how frequent your contractions are, and then I'll check to see how many centimetres you're dilated. I was told that your waters have already broken, is that right?'

'Yes, at around five-thirty am,' I said, bracing myself as another contraction hit.

'Have you had anything to eat or drink, Rebecca?'

'Nothing to eat,' I replied. 'Just a cup of raspberry tea.'

'Well let's have a look at how frequent your contractions are, and then I will get the appropriate paperwork for you to sign. There will be a delivery nurse joining us today. Her name is Lawan. She has worked at the hospital for three years and she has a lot of experience, so you will be in safe hands.'

Minutes blended into hours, and I was in the throes of pushing new life into the world when my mum walked in, just in time to see her first grandson born.

I looked at our baby boy, at his soft, pure skin, his eyes squinting as he adjusted to his new surroundings, and we all cried tears of joy. I had never felt a rush of love like it in my life and I knew in that instant that I would do anything to protect him.

'Welcome to the world, Chadd Carter.' I said as I snuggled him in the crook of my arm, a feeling of complete happiness wrapping itself around us both.

I stayed in hospital for three nights and I enjoyed the special bonding time that I had with my baby boy. He slept most of the first day, but I could not. I was so overawed by him and couldn't stop looking at him lying in his crib. By day three, he was opening his eyes and looking straight at me, searching for food, stretching and wriggling in his doll like baby clothes. I couldn't believe how perfect he was, from the blonde fuzzy hair on his head to his tiny fingernails. He was beyond amazing.

When we arrived home, I was stunned to see that friends and neighbours had brought a variety of gifts, and even those who had so little had rustled up a meal; I was overwhelmed with people's generosity.

We settled into a routine, with Chadd waking every three to four hours for a feed, and, once a week Elanor would offer to do a night feed to give me a break, so I could catch up on some sleep. My mum took Chadd for a walk in his stroller each morning and I sat on the veranda pinching myself, still shocked at the complete turnaround in my life. I still had days when I struggled, when nightmares haunted my sleep until the early hours. On those days, I was so grateful for the support I received from Luke and my family. I tried not to dwell on those times, even though it felt like trawling through mud some days; but what spurred me on was the love of those close to me, and the realization that there could have been an alternative; I could have still been in that house. I could have been dead.

Mum stayed for four weeks and then returned to the UK, but we Skyped twice a week. Life was good.

Chadd was five months old now and he was smiling and telling baby babble stories to anyone that would listen. He always had a willing audience. He was the most beautiful baby, and everyone wanted to stop and talk to him. We had our daily routine after Luke had left for work, and today as usual, I shouted out to Elanor to tell her that I was taking Chadd to the beach.

'I won't be too long and don't worry, he has sunscreen on and his sunhat.' I laughed to myself thinking that my baby had not one, but two protective mothers.

I walked the few metres onto the beach and juggled Chadd in one arm as I flicked the beach mat onto the sand and unhooked the baby bag from my back. We sat down and I took out his books and propped him on my lap as I pointed to pictures and bounced him on my knee, lifting him into the air and kissing his chubby face, watching dimples form as he lapped up the attention.

Back in the house, I gave him a drink of water and put him down for his morning nap.

'I'm going to my bedroom to read while Chadd has a nap, Elanor.'

I picked up my book and started reading, feeling my eyes get heavy with a combination of sleep deprivation, heat, and humidity. I wake with a start and walk out of my room and into Chadd's nursery.

'Elanor!' I shout.

'We're in here, honey.'

Chadd was in his highchair sucking on some pureed fruit that was inside his nubi feeder. He grinned a gummy grin when he saw me and started waving his arms about.

'I must have been more tired than I thought. Thanks for looking after him.' I said, as I nuzzled my son's cheeks.

'Oh, this came while you slept, it was left on the porch,' Elanor handed me a gift box.

I looked at the white box trimmed with blue and secured with a thick navy bow. I opened it up and the most adorable Ralph Lauren baby romper and cardigan were wrapped inside white tissue.

'Wow, mum must have bought this,' I said, holding the items up for Elanor to see. 'They're almost too beautiful to wear and very out of place here, but they are gorgeous.' A part of me felt annoyed that mum would spend that much money on an outfit.

There was a sealed small envelope underneath the branded tissue paper, which I opened.

Congratulations on the birth of your baby boy. Love from Uncle Pez. It read.

And that was the moment that my past caught up with me, and time stood still.

ONE

Dani

I ran out of the door, and I heard Elanor shout after me. I looked back to see my son's eyes following me, wondering if this was some sort of game; and I could see Elanor's mouth moving but the sound was drowned out by the noise of fear pulsing in my head. I ran along the beach towards the rocks, where Luke was fishing; sand flicking up as I sprinted for my life, aware of people stopping and staring, wondering what my hurry was. I could not stop though until I reached Luke.

As I ran, I looked around and I wondered if HE was here now, watching me and laughing. I was terrified that he would walk onto the beach and grab me, while others looked on, allowing him to do whatever he wanted. He had in the past, so there was nothing to stop him now.

The rocks were only metres away now, but I could not see anyone. I started to shout in panic as visuals played out in my head spurring me to imagine that Luke had already been taken by Pez, my punishment for not paying my debt. A life without my best friend and soul mate. No father for Chadd. Panic rose within me like a phoenix from a fire, and I started yelling his name as loud as I could.

'Luke!' I stopped and collapsed onto the sand and sobbed out some my fear and shock. My worst nightmare had come true. Finally, Pez had caught up with us.

I was aware of waves starting to lap around my legs and I wondered how long I had been sat, time slipping through the hourglass without me being aware of it, while I had been trapped inside my past again, struggling to break free.

I forced myself up onto legs that no longer felt solid, and I noticed an old man standing close to me looking concerned. He was dressed in shorts and a vest, and he was wearing a cap. He nodded and took a step towards me, but then hesitated.

'I'm okay,' I said, even though I was far from it. He smiled and nodded and walked the other way, probably relieved that the crazy woman was up on her feet. I ran at a slower pace now until I hit the water. The adrenalin that had powered me eased slightly. Waves slapped up against me, splashing my face as I made my way to the other side of the rocks, and then I saw him and my heart lurched, and a cry escaped my mouth.

'Luke, Oh God Luke.' I said in desperation. He dropped his rod, brow furrowed in confusion and concern as he scrambled over rocks towards me.

'Dani what the hell is wrong? Why are you wading through water looking as if a ghost has chased you along the beach?' He reached out a hand to pull me up.

'It has,' I said in a whisper, before bursting into tears and clinging on to him for dear life, hiccupping words out that were undecipherable. He held me to him silently, allowing me time, and I knew what he was thinking, *it's the post-traumatic stress.* Often, I had nightmares and woke up and ran out onto the beach. I needed to feel sand beneath my toes to remind me that the images in my head were not real, that they were part of my former life that could no longer hurt me. This time however, the sand beneath my feet was not a comfort and it did not make me feel safe, because there was no escaping the past now that it had come knocking on my door.

Luke sat down next to me with his arm around my back, and he pulled my head into his shoulder. I looked at the sea pounding out the same rhythm that it churned every day, and I cried again because nothing felt certain anymore. I looked at Luke, and my heart skipped a beat, it was one of those moments when your love for someone knocks the breath out of you. I couldn't imagine my life without him, but I knew that even if we paid the money back to Pez, it wouldn't be enough.

'Do you want to talk now?' he asked me gently, wiping the tears that fell out of my swollen eyes. I couldn't even begin to form words, so I just handed him the now crumpled and damp gift card. He read the words and I watched the colour drain from his sun-kissed face and fear take over, turning him into another person.

'Fuck no!' he said in a panic, standing up, as he pulled his hands through his hair and paced back and forward on top of the large rock.

'Where is Chadd, Dani?' He asked desperately, as he looked in the direction our house.

'It's fine, he's with Elanor,' I said, but my words fizzled out when it registered that while I'd been sprinting along the beach, anything could have happened to him. I was off again with Luke already way ahead and running at a much faster pace. Again, people around us were wondering what was happening, looking along the beach searching for signs of a commotion.

Luke reached the house before me and by the time I got there he was holding Chadd in his arms on the veranda. I looked around as I took my baby boy from him and wrapped myself around him protectively, I felt as if there were eyes in the trees that lined the beach behind our house, and I felt the need for a drink calling me, another friend from the past that I had thought was dead and buried. Anxiety ate away at my insides, making me feel hyper-vigilant. Elanor hovered in the background waiting for an explanation.

'Would you mind telling me what is going on you two, you're starting to scare me.' Elanor said.

My eyes flicked to Luke's and time froze for a few seconds. Luke sighed and asked Elanor to sit down, and like me he had no words to explain, so he handed her the card. Her mouth fell open and she looked between us as the realization hit her.

'Oh. I. I am lost for words. I just don't know what to say other than I'm scared for both of you, for Chadd; for all of us.' She wrung her hands together and stood up, 'Excuse me please, I need a moment alone.'

I watched her shakily make her way out of the room. Luke and I sat opposite each other; silence and shock surrounding us like an invisible bubble.

'She needs time,' Luke said. 'We'll check on her in if she's not back in fifteen minutes. Knowing Elanor, she'll want to have a good cry alone.' I nodded, holding my precious boy close to me, afraid to put him down or let him out of my sight in case he disappeared.

'What are we going to do Luke?' I was aware that he didn't have all the answers, but I needed to start formulating some kind of plan.

'We need to move from here that much I do know, but where to? Do we stay in Thailand or go somewhere else?' he asked me.

'I feel sick. It's like someone has delivered a ticking bomb that will follow us wherever we go, and we have no way of knowing when it will go off. I'm worried for all of us, even for Elanor.'

As if on cue Elanor walked back into the room. 'I'm sorry. It was such a shock, thinking that he knows where we live now. We have to leave, today. I called your mum, Dani, and she will pay for one month's rent here in advance, just let the landlord know and you two decide where we go next.'

As confronting as it was to think of moving again, I was pleased that Elanor was taking control because Luke and I were drowning in our own fear.

'I think we should get a flight to one of the other islands and then we can check into a hotel for a couple of days and give ourselves time to think properly.' Luke said.

'Can you go online and book some flights out of here now Luke? I really want to leave as soon as possible. I don't feel safe and I'm terrified that someone might storm through that door at any minute.' Elanor's voice wobbled with emotion.

I walked into Chadd's room and placed him in his cot, the beautiful cot that I would have to leave behind for now, maybe forever. Sadness washed over me as I grabbed all his clothes and bundled them into a suitcase. I placed his photo album on top of the clothes.

'Can you get me a box from the garage please, Elanor?'

'What are you doing Dani?' She asked, gently, as she placed her hand on my shoulder.

'I'm going to ask Joe if he minds keeping one or two boxes for me in his garage. I'll say that my mum is unwell and that we need to go away for a while. I'm putting all of the gifts that Chadd received in here, and some books my dad bought me. I can always pay Joe to send them on. I'm frightened to leave them here just in case soemone trashes the place.'

'Good thinking honey. We'll be in the lounge.' She picked Chadd out of his cot. 'I'll get our passports together and see how Luke is getting on while you finish packing.'

'Thanks El.' I sat down on the rocking chair and looked around at the nursery. Anger surged through me when I thought about how far I had come. Earlier today I was sat on the beach with Chadd, talking to him, reading him stories, and now here we were having our lives turned upside down again; back to living life on the edge, twenty-four seven, with no respite from the fear.

Luke walked into the room fifteen minutes later. 'I've booked us one-way flights to Koh Samui, and two rooms in a hotel next to the beach. We can decide what we need to do once we get there.' He kissed me on the forehead and wrapped his arms around me; arms that no longer felt safe. 'We need to finish packing Dani because our flight leaves in less than four hours.'

'I'm almost done in here. Can you pack basics for me, shorts, t-shirts etc... and I'll call next door to see Joe and ask him to keep these boxes.'

Thirty minutes later we all got into a taxi, and I looked back at the house that has been our home for the past eighteen months, and I already felt as if I was mourning what we had to leave behind.

Two

Luke

I was lost in my own world looking out to sea, fishing rod in hand, when Dani appeared thigh-high in water. At first, I thought it was one of her crazy jokes, because she did have a wicked sense of humour, but then I saw the look of terror on her face and the frantic pace as she tried to navigate the waves that were crashing against her, pushing her up against the rocks. Her breathing was laboured and erratic. I had seen this many times when her past caught up with her. She had flashbacks, which seemed to lessen in frequency but grow in intensity. I rushed to comfort her because she was distraught, and I hugged her to me as she garbled words in between sobs. I couldn't make out anything she was saying, so I waited until she calmed down. I'd not seen her this distressed in a long time, and I wondered what had happened to trigger such a reaction.

'Do you want to talk now?' I asked her gently. She looked at me, silently talking to me with eyes as deep as the ocean; eyes that always reached out to me, as if she was inaudibly begging for help. Her breathing changed and she seemed stuck somehow, unable to function as her words hit an invisible force field that denied them life. She handed me a crumpled card that read: *Congratulations on the birth of your baby boy. Love from Uncle Pez.*

I froze for a few seconds as my brain registered the words, and then I went into overdrive.

'Dani where's Chadd?' I asked her urgently because I could see that she was in crisis mode. I didn't wait for a reply because adrenalin took over and I was sprinting along the beach giving Ussain Bolt a run for his money. I flew into the house, half expecting to find an empty cot, but relief flooded through me as I saw Elanor sitting on the floor with Chadd, playing with toys. She stood when I entered.

'Thank Fuck.' I said, as I scooped my son into my arms and cradled him to me protectively. Elanor raised an eyebrow in disapproval of my language.

'What's going on Luke? Dani took off like a rocket along the beach and now you're flying in here in a panic?' Elanor queried, concern etched on her face.

'I'll tell you in a minute Elanor.'

Dani came up the steps and took Chadd from me. Elanor was sandwiched between us, eyes darting from my face to Dani's, so I handed her the card. Like Dani, I could not find the words to explain what I was feeling right now and the words I needed to say stuck in my throat. I was unable to think clearly as flashbacks of Gunner raining blows down on me had me on edge. I was half expecting him to walk through the door at any minute, grinning at the thought of an encore. I snapped back to the present as Elanor asked me to book flights out of Phuket, and I was glad of something concrete to do because I felt as if I was trapped in quicksand that was drawing me in with the intent of suffocating me.

'Where's the box that the clothes came in Dani?' I asked. 'Did you notice if there was a stamp on the packaging? Was it mailed or hand delivered?'

'I didn't even think to look to be honest. I just ripped the paper off and took the clothes out, I thought it was from mum at first, and then I legged it out of the house to find you.'

I took the wrapping out of the bin and there were no stamps on it. Fuck! That meant that the gift had been hand delivered, and it meant that Pez or one of his men had been here, at our house!

Twenty minutes later Dani, Chadd, Elanor, and I crammed into a cab on our way to the airport. My senses were suddenly awakened as I took in the traffic that surrounded us. Eyes searching for a car that stood out as my heart thumped an uneven rhythm in my chest.

We arrived at the airport and checked our luggage in and I see that Dani is struggling to keep it together. We find a seat and Elanor pushes Chadd in his buggy, showing him different things to keep him entertained.

'Dani, I know it's hard but try to stay calm. The last thing we want is to draw attention to ourselves.' I said quietly. 'If you break down here it will cause a fuss, and we're trying to keep a low profile.'

She faltered, eyes filling with tears, and she talked just above a whisper.

'I can't control how I feel Luke. I feel as if an evil spirit is following us around.' Her breathing is shallow and her skin is pale.

'If he comes after anyone it will be me; you and Chadd are safe. Think about it, what would Pez do with a baby? You know him, and he's all about himself, babies aren't his style. And once we get to Koh Sam we can call your mum and then things will feel much clearer, she will know what to do.' I soothed.

'This means we have to spend the rest of our lives looking over our shoulder Luke. I won't ever feel able to let Chadd run around in the garden or cycle up and down the street while I prepare dinner, you know, normal things that kids do. He's going to live such a restricted life without knowing why.'

'That depends where we live. There are ways around this and you're letting your mind race too far ahead into the future. It's no use stressing about things that haven't happened yet. One day at a time remember. It's almost time to board the plane. We'll be out of here before you know it.'

I didn't have the heart to admit that I was just as terrified as her.

THREE

Eva

I looked at the mail that lay scattered across the mat and groaned as I scooped it off the floor; creaking knees a reminder that I was not getting any younger. My eyes fell upon a brown envelope with the words **Do Not Bend,** written across in black marker. I walked to the dresser and picked up the hand carved paper knife which had belonged to my father, and I slipped it in between the seal creating a perfect opening. I picked out half a dozen photographs. The first one was a picture of Dani and Chadd on the beach. The wind had gently whipped the hair off Dani's face and her natural beauty caught me off-guard.

There had been such a positive change in Dani since she fell pregnant with the baby. She had really looked after herself, and I was convinced that being pregnant had aided her stoic recovery from alcoholism. Both Dani and Luke had worked hard to make their relationship work and I couldn't fault the support that Luke had given her. I was proud of them both, and despite my initial dislike of Luke, I was now very fond of him.

There were five other pictures, all similar in the sense that they were taken from an angle. The final picture was of Elanor and Luke talking on the veranda, Elanor was holding Chadd in her arms. I found it odd that there was no full-face pictures of Dani or Chadd, but nonetheless I was overjoyed to see my daughter and grandson. I placed the photographs back on the table and planned to thank

Dani when I phoned her later. Right now, I had a charity event to attend to raise money for the rape crisis centre in London.

Later that afternoon I left the event feeling elated that we had raised a total of fifteen thousand pounds. That would help pay towards an additional counsellor for the centre. It was a drop in the ocean considering the need, but it still felt good to contribute, and the fund raising would continue.

I reached into my bag to turn my phone on, and a succession of missed calls chimed through from Elanor. I looked at my watch and realized that she had called me five times within three minutes. I dialed her number wondering what was so urgent while trying not to let my mind catastrophize.

'Elanor is everything OK. Sorry I've been to the charity event I was telling you about.'

'Oh Eva, it's awful, I'm so upset.' She gushed in an emotional voice. I could tell that she had been crying and it sounded as if she was on the verge of more tears. My mind went into overdrive.

'Dani received a gift today, Eva. A Ralph Lauren outfit for Chadd and at first we thought it was from you.' She was sobbing down the phone now. What on earth was going on? How could a designer gift be such a problem?

'Elanor what has happened for goodness' sake, this is confusing and worrying. Why are you so upset?'

'Sorry Eva. Give me a moment.' I heard her blow her nose and take a deep breath. 'There was a gift tag with the outfit,' she spoke quietly, and a feeling of dread shrouded me as I waited for the punch line. 'It said *Congratulations on the birth of your baby boy. Love from Uncle Pez.*'

Nothing on earth could have prepared me for the words that had just filtered through the phone. I felt the air leave my body in a rush as dizziness knocked me off balance.

'How on earth has he found them? We have to do something Elanor. You must get out of there as soon as possible. Take what you need and tell Luke to book flights to another part of Thailand, or Singapore, anywhere that will give us all some breathing space to figure out what to do from here.'

'I'll speak to them now. I'm so scared for their safety. I'll go, Eva, because I need to talk to Dani and Luke.' She said hurriedly, anxiety building in her voice. I swallowed down my terror, but it came back up.

'Keep me up to date with what's happening please and in the meantime I will try and think of something to keep you all safe.' I ended the call and sat in the car racking my brains about what they could do next. The reality was, I had no idea *how* to help them anymore.

Once home, I sat down heavily on the sofa. I was unable to think straight, so I walked into my bedroom and took out the brown bottle of diazepam that the doctor had prescribed me when Dani was in rehab. The doctor wasn't aware that Dani had ever been found of course, and it had been a long time since I had relied on these tablets, but right now I was in desperate need of calming myself and numbing the terror that I felt. I popped one full tablet into my mouth, and I lay on top of the bed and closed my eyes, willing my body to sleep and relax, even if only for a short while.

I woke an hour later with the familiar feeling of a hazy drug detached brain. The intense anxiety had been reduced with a Perspex wall now placed between my thoughts and feelings. I was able to think about the situation without experiencing the extreme bodily reactions; no heart thumping or icy adrenalin flying through my system like an out-of-control high speed car. Ironically, I understood how difficult it must be for people to stop taking drugs, especially if their lives were full of stress.

My phone jingled its ring tone and I quickly swiped to answer it.

'Darling girl, how are you?' I asked; and despite the tablet, I could feel emotion swimming to the surface. I imagined the terror Dani must have felt when she read the words on that gift tag, and how her past must have crashed through to the present.

'Oh mum, I don't know what we are going to do,' she sobbed, and my heart broke for her. 'I'm terrified that they have come back for me and Luke, and what about Chadd and Elanor.'

I closed my eyes trying to summon a brilliant idea. 'Has Luke booked flights darling?' I asked.

'Yes, we're flying to Koh Samui in a couple of hours but I don't know what we do beyond that.' Her desperation was evident. I pictured her beautiful face, pale, and etched with anxiety, and all I wanted was for her to be able to live her life without fear.

'Well give me tonight to think of something. Between Luke and I, we will come up with a plan, don't worry. Oh, and thank you for the photographs. Chadd has grown so much since last month.' I added quickly in a bid to lighten the mood.

'What photographs mum?' she asked in alarm.

'The ones you sent me in the post. I received them today.'

'Mum, I have not sent you any photographs!'

She yelled out to Elanor and Luke asking them if they had posted any photographs to me. I heard them confirm that they had not.

'Are the photographs of me mum?' Her voice raising to a high-pitched squeak.

'There are five in total, four of you with Chadd, and one of Elanor and Luke standing on the veranda,' I said in a whisper, and ice shifted through my veins at the realization that they had been watched.

'Oh God he's playing cat and mouse with us.' Dani choked as a sob caught in her throat. My heart lurched in my chest as I realized that the game had just taken on a new level.

'Dani, you need to keep it together darling. Get to the airport as soon as you can, you will be safe there and then check into your hotel and text me, I will call you as soon as you get there.'

'Okay, I'm so scared though.' She said, sounding every bit as vulnerable as a child.

'I know darling, me too, but there has to be a way around this. Now go to the airport and I'll speak to you soon.'

As I end the call I burst into tears, the enormity of this situation hits me. I have some big decisions to make and I have to make them soon, before it was too late.

Four

Dani

The airport was overwhelmingly noisy. Chatter of different languages filled the air and the overly loud tannoy screamed to life every few seconds, blasting out a burst of Thai words, followed by a broken English version that was hard to decipher amongst the overall racket. Cheap perfume and deodorant burned my nostrils, and I felt like sitting on the floor and crying until someone came and rescued me.

I was shaking and anxious, and wherever I looked around me there was a wall of security to get through. This was both good and bad. Good because it would mean once I was through customs I could relax for a few hours, and bad because I was anxious and stressed and I had lost my ability to think straight. I pictured myself in a Bridget Jones style scenario, handcuffed and led away – blown in by Pez for having a false identity, *the missing girl arrested for identity theft at Thai airport.*

I scanned the space around me looking for Pez, but the faces all blurred into each other, and the room felt as if it was spinning. I took a deep breath, trying to gain some composure and perspective, but nothing seemed to be working and the adrenalin continued to course through my veins at an alarming rate.

We slowly make our way to the kiosk to check-in after what felt like a five-hour wait in the queue, but in reality, it was twenty minutes. A sophisticated and very pretty Thai lady behind the blue desk looked at my passport and then at me. She smiled but continued to flick her eyes between the two, before typing something into the computer screen that was hidden from my view. I could feel sweat forming on my top lip, and I wondered what the problem was. Luke touched my arm causing me to jump.

'Babe, come on let's go.' I realized that the lady was handing me back the passports with the black and white airlines tickets slotted neatly inside. I grabbed them quickly and thanked her as relief flooded through me.

I spent the next sixty minutes nervously waiting to board the plane. Thankfully there was no sign of Pez and I was starting to think that he had sent someone else to tail us.

Finally, we walked on to the plane and I took my seat strapping myself in as tightly as possible, a reminder that I was safe, for now. I relished the quiet of the plane in comparison to the crazy airport as we soared into the sky, anxiety slipping away as we ascended.

I gazed out of the window below at the turquoise green water that surrounded the islands, and the ocean that separated like torn paper as boats steamed through it. Glimpses of white sand stood out against the contrast of rock and greenery, selling the pictures of paradise that adorned travel brochures across the world.

'What will we do Luke?' I searched his face looking for reassurance and safety, but all I saw was a mirror image of how I felt.

'Dani, I...' He stalled, looking for words to fill the gaps. 'Your mum is doing what she can and I'm hoping that by the time we land and check in to the hotel, she will have something arranged for us.'

'But it means moving again, starting over, and living where?' I asked, frantically.

'What other option do we have Dani? We can't just live a normal life now, you know that.' He closed his eyes, most likely trying to escape the barrage of questions I kept firing at him. I thought about our future and wondered what it might look like; I wondered if we would be moving from caravan parks to motels, as an invisible shadow followed us; or would we end up living in the middle of nowhere, in some hot foreign country where flies swarmed around you and dust devils tore up the ground before disappearing without trace.

I closed my eyes in a bid to stop the tears that begged to flow and I looked at our son, fast asleep in my arms, an innocent victim in this game that Pez was playing, and I wondered when our time would be up, and what would happen to my precious baby.

We arrived in Koh Samui and the heat hit me in the face as I stepped off the small plane onto the ground. I looked around and saw an open-air space with a carousel and not much else. It felt so different compared to the airport we had just come from, and fear swelled within me as I realized how vulnerable we were in this open unmanned space.

Luke grabbed a trolley for our luggage, which arrived within seconds, and we walked up a ramp towards the taxi drivers who were all shouting for a fare. Luke booked us onto a shuttle bus, and I breathed another small sigh of relief as we buckled up and closed the door, grateful for the air conditioning that caressed our faces and sticky bodies.

Twenty minutes later we arrived at the Fisherman's Village and walked into the hotel reception that smelled of fresh lemons, and frangipani. The walls were adorned with gilded mirrors and carved dark wooden furniture stood solidly on the cream marble floors. Staff in matching beige and gold uniforms bowed and greeted us with warm smiles and welcomes.

'Dani I'll unpack and then take Chadd for a walk around the hotel grounds.' Elanor said as she touched my arm affectionately. 'You and Luke have a lot to talk about and you should ring your mum to let her know that we arrived safely.'

'Thanks Elanor.' As ever, I wondered what I would do without her.

Luke swiped the key into our room, and I put Chadd on the bed. He was chuckling to himself, unaware of the precarious situation that we were all in. I thanked God that he was not older and able to ask questions about why we were suddenly moving. I lay down next to him against the cool, soft white sheets, relieved that we had all managed to get out of Phuket unscathed. Exhaustion overwhelmed me and my lids grew heavy as I shut out the sounds of suitcases wheeling along the corridor and jet ski's in the distance.

I woke an hour later to hear Luke's voice drifting through the room from the bathroom. I sat up on the pillow and tried to shake the sleep from my foggy head, forgetting momentarily why I was in a strange room, feeling a punch in my chest when I remembered.

I could hear Luke's muffled talk and it sounded as if he was speaking to my mum. I padded across the cold tiles and put my ear to the wooden door.

'Eva, you don't have a choice, you were sent the pictures as a warning.' I hear him say. 'A warning that they know where you live and a message that they have been watching us all.' I push the door and watch him pacing the floor, tense and agitated, he looks momentarily shocked to see me, almost as if he'd forgotten I was in the same room. 'Call him,' he says, before agreeing to speak to my mum again in the morning.

I waited for him to talk to me, reassure me and tell me that there's some kind of plan in place, that everything would be okay, but he looked at the floor, avoiding eye contact.

'Luke?' He cleared his throat and shuffled his feet, glancing at me without holding eye contact for more than a few seconds. 'What did mum say? What happens next?' I question. Seconds passed by like minutes.

'Your mum needs a little more time babe. She's trying to contact Ameen but he's not answered yet.'

'So, there is no plan right at this moment?' I can feel hysteria building momentum inside of me. 'We have no plan. We just stay here and wait for him to come and get us?' I shout.

'For fuck's sake Dani, calm down.' Luke steered me on to the bed. The urge to have a drink was overwhelming, and I eyed the mini bar that sat behind the slatted wooden doors, and Luke caught me staring.

'No!' He said firmly, staring me down. 'That's not the answer Dani!' He got up and took out the alcohol that called my name, and poured it down the sink, and I felt relief flood through me because now the temptation has been removed. I plaited my hair and tapped my feet as the cloak of anxiety wrapped itself around me.

'I need air.' I said, and walked out of the room, unsure of where I was going.

The heat of the day hit me full force as I made my way towards the beachfront. I looked around at the people that were here on holiday, and I envied them so much it hurt inside. They had nothing to fear other than how much food they might overindulge in, or how much alcohol they might drink. They would leave their holiday and return to their normal lives and jobs, and never know what it felt like to live in terror of a past hunting you down. They would never know the pain of reliving your past trauma on a nightly basis, something that was now awakened thanks to that clothes parcel and that bastard man.

I remove my flip-flops; the hot sand was unpleasant to walk on as I made my way towards the ocean. The beach was quiet apart from a few hotel guests sunbathing near the hotel steps, so I put a little distance between myself and them and I sat down on the damp sand, allowing the warm water to soothe my feet as the waves gently advanced and retreated.

Sometime later, Luke sat down next to me and slipped his arm around me before kissing me on the cheek. Silent tears rolled out of my eyes as emotion swelled in my chest.

'It's going to be OK baby, I promise you. It's going to be OK.' Luke said, and I clung to his words because they were the only anchor that was saving me from drowning in my own fear right now.

FIVE

Eva

Eva

I drove straight to Peter's house and pressed the tannoy on the gate. '*Peter it's me, please let me in*,' I shouted at the metal box, while a beige marble lion looked down at me.

The gate buzzed to life gliding slowly past my vision allowing me into the grounds, the grounds where we drugged the obese man and smuggled Dani out of the country. It seemed a lifetime ago; a lifetime that has now come back to haunt us all.

Peter was stood outside of his door waiting for me. 'What on earth is wrong Eva?' he asked, stepping down the stairs of the entrance. As ever he looked effortlessly refined in navy trousers and a white short-sleeved shirt, and despite his wealth and love of fine foods, somehow, he managed to retain his physique and stay slim.

I ran up the steps grabbing him, terrified that we are being watched. 'Quickly inside Peter.' I said, looking behind me as I rushed past him urging him to follow. He looked at me concerned but did as requested; checking beyond the entrance to his property, no doubt wondering what invisible terror I was running from.

'Can I have a drink please?' I asked.

Peter opened his mouth as if about to talk, but then shook his head in confusion before leaving the room. I needed time to calm myself and I hadn't really thought through how much information to give him. I wasn't even sure if I could trust him, but I was rapidly running out of options and time.

Peter walked back into the room with a tray, and ever the host, there was an array of options from a pot of tea, to iced water and a gin and tonic. I grabbed the water and gulped it down, even though the gin and tonic would have been preferable.

'Peter, I need you to sit down and listen to me because I have something to tell you that will shock you.' I was aware that I was mimicking the words that Luke had said to me almost two years earlier. 'I need your help, and I need you to trust that the least you know the better for your own wellbeing.'

His eyes widened momentarily. 'Eva, have you banged your head or are you feeling unwell? You're not making a lot of sense at the minute if I'm honest with you.'

I put my head in my hands and all of the worry and emotion rushed out of me; tears rolled down my face, and a wail of despair pushed out of my mouth without permission. Peter rushed over and comforted me, confused at my dishevelled, hysterical behaviour.

'What is it Eva? What on earth is wrong?' he asked, visibly shaken as he caressed my hand.

'Oh, Peter, it's ... it's all such a mess and I'm not sure where to turn or what to do. Excuse me while I pop to the bathroom, and then I promise that I will tell you what I can.'

'Of course.' He said kindly, as his eyes followed me out of the room.

I splashed my face with cold water and dabbed it dry with the soft white towel that smelled of rosewater. I took some deep breaths in a bid to compose myself before entering the room.

'Sorry, I know this is confusing for you and it's hard for me to even begin to say what has happened, so I am just going to say it.'

Peter was staring at me nervously, nodding silently as if to urge me on.

'The thing is, Dani is still alive and well, in fact she now has a baby and she has been living overseas for the past eighteen months or so. She had to leave the country for her own safety, and Luke's.' I add, aware that I have been speaking at one hundred miles an hour, and I force myself to look at him. The look of shock on his face is staggering. 'Please understand Peter, I couldn't say anything. Dani and Luke are in some trouble, danger actually, and I need your, I need someone's help.' I'm struggling to make eye contact with him for more than a second or two at a time, and my cheeks are flushed with guilt and embarrassment.

'What kind of help exactly?' He asked, warily, when he finally found his voice.

'I need help arranging for Luke, Dani and the baby to move country.' I was aware that my request on a scale of one to ten, sat at around one thousand.

'Move country!' He stated incredulously. 'You can't just move country on a whim Eva, and why on earth do they need to move? Why can't they just come home? And what have they done that is so bad?'

'Quite honestly, they haven't really done anything, all I can say is that Luke got mixed up with some bad people, and Dani did something that upset them, she's young and had no idea of the implications of her actions. These *people* have no rules, they kill people for fun and they are above the law, believe me, you have no idea what they are capable of.' I watched him silently question me with his facial expressions and I knew that he thought I was just behaving like a frenetic parent.

'Just to be clear, because I'm struggling to get my head around all of this Eva, you're telling me that all of this time your daughter has been safe and well, and she is living with the man responsible for her being *missing*, and she now has a baby with him!'

He was agitated. I watched him pacing around the large room, before leaning against the marble fireplace for support. He looked at me as if he had never seen me before in his life.

'I know this is a lot to take in and I understand if you are angry with me,' I said, 'but please don't tell anyone about anything that I have said to you because this information is confidential, Peter. All their lives are in danger, and most likely mine as well.' I added solemnly.

'So, the police know nothing?' He queried, and I can tell by the look on his face that he already knows the answer and disagrees with me.

'No and they can never know because like I say, these people are above the law.'

'But that's ridiculous Eva. How can they be for goodness' sake? You're not living in America in the fifties in some gangster movie! I don't understand at all and frankly, I think you should go to the police today if you fear for their safety, and yours!' he said firmly.

'You're not listening to me Peter,' I said in a diminishing voice, because any hope I had of him helping was fading rapidly.

'Oh, I am listening Eva, and what I hear is that you have lied to police and all of your friends. I've been with you when people have comforted you and offered support about your missing, now presumed dead daughter, and you have sat there and acted out your role like a pro. I don't know who you are anymore, and it makes me wonder what else you have hidden from me during our relationship!'

'Do you think I had a choice?' I yell at him, desperately wanting him to understand. 'My daughter was kidnapped and held hostage in a house and FORCED to entertain men for months on end, day in, day out! She was beaten and raped! Luke was beaten, and they cut one of his fingers off and left him for dead, and one of his friends that helped them escape was murdered not long after they left the country! *Now,* now do you understand why I cannot put myself or my family in a position of trying to fight these people?' I felt weak with anxiety and emotion, and I wanted to curl up into a ball and stay there forever.

Peter opened his mouth and then closed it, before sitting down heavily on a chair. A sig of air escaped his lips. 'Eva, I ... I don't know what to say.' He seemed to be shaking.

'It's OK Peter. You don't have to say anything. I'm sorry for bringing this to your door. I was lost and had nowhere else to turn and it's such a lot to absorb I know. I've been in your position the day that Luke showed up and told me where Dani was.'

He shook his head in disbelief at the enormity of the words that had most likely changed our relationship forever, and not in a positive way.

'As I was saying, they have been living quite happily, just getting on with their life, working, and looking after the baby. I received some pictures recently. Pictures of Dani and the baby.' I hand them to him. 'I thought the pictures were odd because they were taken from a strange angle. Then Elanor rang me to tell me that Dani had received a gift for the baby, only the gift was from the man that had held Dani hostage. When I spoke to Dani, she confirmed that she had not sent me the photographs, so clearly it is a message to let me know that they are watching

Dani, and they know where I live. I'm frightened Peter and I don't know what to do.' I sobbed.

'Well, I'd say the first thing you need to do is move! If these people are as dangerous as you say, then you can't mess around Eva. Put your house up for sale, it's too big for a single woman living alone anyway.'

I looked around at the vast house that Peter lived in, and opened my mouth to protest, but thought better of it.

'My immediate issue is rehoming Dani and her family. They're staying in a hotel, but obviously they can't stay there indefinitely. I need them to disappear, and they need new identities.' I add. I had told Peter far more than I had intended.

'Eva, I don't have those kind of powers, I don't even know how to get a new identity and as much as I care for you, I cannot break the law.'

'You have contacts with your business in other countries, Peter. You could give Luke a job and that would allow them to leave Thailand and start over, somewhere safe.' I pleaded, more than asked him.

'What happens if they move and get found again?'

I chose to ignore his question because I had no way of answering it. 'I know this is a lot to ask, but please, will you at least think about it?

Peter walked the floor again and barely left a footprint in the plush cream carpet.

'I will think about it overnight Eva, but please don't put too much onus on me at present, because at this point in time I am not promising anything.'

'Thank you,' I said, as I hugged him, and despite what he had said, I *was* pinning all of my hopes on him, because I had no other option.

I had a very sleepless night, wondering what Peter's decision would be, my mind churning over what I would do if he decided against helping. I woke before sunrise and I made myself a cup of camomile tea in a weak bid to help reduce my stress levels. I was tempted to reach for the bottle of diazepam, but I knew that

I needed to have a clear head when I spoke to Peter, and then I needed to talk to Luke and Dani. I only hoped when I did, that that I had something constructive to say to them.

I looked out of the window at the sun rising and I wondered how many people were starting their day worrying about what they would cook for dinner, if it might rain if they hang washing out, or whether to mow the lawn; I wished that my daughter could be one of those people with those level of worries.

I waited until nine am and then I picked the telephone up. I tapped in the numbers, holding my breath as I waited... and waited, before it clicked in to voice mail. I slammed the phone down unsure of what to say. Fear rose within me as I wondered whether Peter would go to the police with the information I had shared with him. The phone trilled to life making me jump.

'It's Peter, Eva, how are you feeling this morning?'

'Peter. I'm so relieved to hear your voice. I thought, well I thought that you might never want to speak to me again.' I said nervously.

'As tempting as this may be, I care for you and I have thought about nothing else since you left yesterday. I do have an idea about how I could help, but there are several obstacles in the way and I need to discuss them with you, are you able to come over to my house later this morning? I have a few calls to make so give me an hour.'

'Of course. Thank you.'

I put the phone down and cried, the pent-up stress running out of me like a river bursting its banks.

I took a shower and put some make up on to attempt to hide my tired, swollen eyes.

Peter was waiting for me as I parked the car, and he gave me a hug as I entered his house.

'Have a seat Eva,' he said, and I gently perched myself on the sofa. 'As I said to you over the phone, I have some things worked out but not others, but I can see that I might be able to help. I won't say it was an easy decision and if anything comes back onto me, I will simply claim I knew nothing about the *illegal* stuff. I'm prepared to help, but I'm not prepared to put my business or reputation at risk.'

I felt detached as I waited for him to tell me what his plan was. He poured himself a coffee and cleared his throat in a determined, business-like way.

'As you know, I have a global business, so I do see an opportunity for me to create a job for Luke. There are two problems that I envisage, the first being that the job would be in Australia, and the second would be that they would need a visa, and I am not getting involved in anything to do with fake passports, so that side of things I will be blind to. I am prepared to offer work to Luke but I am not contacting anyone or dealing with anything unsavoury. That's as good as I can do Eva.'

'Australia is so far.'

'It's a vast country and even if this man ever found out that they were living there, the chances of him finding them would be a million to one. They will get to live the life that they want to in Australia. They can have the suburban dream without fear of being tracked down.'

'When you put it like that,' I said, feeling very conflicted. On one hand I loved the idea of them having a house, a job, and the opportunity to live a normal life, but on the other, the thought of them being so far away was devastating.

'There are two options.' Peter said, animatedly. 'The first job I could create would be in Queensland, in a town called Rockhampton. The second position would be in New South Wales in a town called Armidale, which is roughly halfway between Brisbane and Sydney.'

'Wow.' Was all I could manage to say.

'You don't seem wowed at all.' Peter stated, disappointment evident in both his voice and his expression.

'I'm sorry. I am truly grateful, it's just the thought of them being so far away.'

'About that Eva,' He paused, and my heart rate spiked. 'I was thinking that maybe it would be better for you to move with them also.'

The words hang in the air like thick fog, blurring my vision. I blinked and tears coursed silently down my cheeks, giving away my shock. It was silly really, but I'd come to love spending time with him, and I enjoyed the time we spent socializing and travelling. The thought of moving to a remote place, knowing no one other than my immediate family and Elanor, filled me with terror.

'I know that you're upset Elanor and believe me the last thing I want is for you to leave. However, if you leaving means that you will be safe, then I have to encourage that, especialy if these people are as bad as you say.'

I knew that what Peter was saying made sense, however I wasn't ready to fully commit to that just yet.

'I'll speak to Luke and let him know the options. Thank you again Peter, you have no idea how thankful I am.'

I kissed him briefly and managed to hold it together until I drove away from his house and a relationship that I valued immensely.

Six

Luke

I answered the phone quietly, praying that Eva had good news.

'Is Dani there with you?' Eva queried.

'Yes, why?'

'Can you go outside? I need to talk to you, but I think it's best if I tell you first and then you can speak to Dani when you've thought about what I have to say. You know how anxious she gets, and I don't want her anymore stressed out than she already is.'

I look at Dani who is outside on the front patio with Chadd. They are pointing to flowers and the birds that fly between the trees. I leave the room and walk down a pathway to a quiet area.

'Okay Eva, I'm outside. Tell me what the go is.' I felt my heart lurch in my chest as I tried to fill in the gaps.

'I met with Peter yesterday,' she said. 'And I'm sorry for not calling afterwards but I needed time to get my head around his suggestion.' She paused and I waited for her to continue. 'To get to the point Luke, Peter suggested that you apply for a working holiday visa for Australia. It only takes a matter of days to get approved, apparently. Once in the country Peter will advertise a management job and he will offer the position to you and then start the sponsorship process which he assures me should be easier with you in the country.'

'And Dani and Chadd?'

' For now Dani will have to apply for a holiday visa, which lasts three months.'

I'm trying to take it all in and I feel as if my head is swimming.

'So, you're saying I have to leave Thailand and go to Australia without Dani and Chadd. Then Dani will come to Australia, but only for three months? Have I got that right Eva because if I have, how the does that help us in the long term?'

'I know this is not ideal, but can you think of an alternative, because if you can feel free to fill me in!' She gushed in annoyance.

'Eva what happens after the three months?'

'Hopefully the visa will be approved before then.'

'It all seems a bit up in the air. I don't want to make such a big move only to find out that three months down the line we have to start over somewhere else.'

'Listen Luke, I understand your reservations, and while there are no guarentees, Peter is confident he can push through a visa for you, and this is the only solution that we can come up with that will give you all an opportunity to have anonymity and safety.'

'Wow. Australia.' I said with a mixture of intrigue and dejection, as the reality started to filter through my brain. 'So what happens next?'

'The first thing you need to do is convince Dani that this move is a good idea, and then you need to apply for your holiday visa. I thought that Dani, Chadd, and Elanor could fly to Singapore with you, and they can book into a hotel for a week or so, and then they can fly on to Australia once you are sorted. What do you think Luke?' Eva asked, and I could hear the fear and desperation in her voice.

'As seems to be the case in our life, I don't think we have any other option other than to go along with it, even though it's crazy. I mean, how are you going to see Chadd? Do you plan to have a holiday every few month or what? How's this going to work Eva?'

'You're not the only one making sacrifices Luke believe me.' She replied emotionally.

Guilt choked me like an invisible rope as I thought about the sacrifices, we all needed to make.

'Here's daddy look.' Dani said, smiling as I walked through the door. 'Where've you been babe?' she asked as she wrestled with a wriggling baby and a press-stud vest.

'I spoke to your mum. Do you want to see if El will take Chadd for a walk and then we can talk about it all.'

She eyed me suspiciously.

'Okay,' she replied hesitantly. 'Give me two minutes and I'll be back.' She kissed Chadd's face before placing him in his stroller and I watched her gather his essentials before hurrying out of the room. I was trying to figure how best to do to sell it to her when she rushed through the door like a whirlwind.

'Tell me Luke. What did mum say?' She demanded urgently.

I cleared my throat, and I plastered on a smile and sat next to her on the bed. I put my arm around her shoulder, pulling her into me so that I did not have to look her directly in the eye.

'Well, it's not as bad as you think babe, so relax, I can see that you're stressed.' I kept going while I was on a roll, hoping that my words didn't sound as enormously life changing as Eva's had. 'Our new destination will still warm your bones through, and it's half-way between here and the UK; sort of anyway. We're going to Australia babe.' There, I'd said it.

Dani pulled away and looked at me as if I had told her that we were going to live on Jupiter.

'God, you're not even joking, are you?' She asked incredulously.

'It's a shock, I know. I felt the same, but think about the positives. Chadd will be safe, and he'll be able to have the childhood we've always wanted him to have. He can go to school, play at the park, and have friends over for play dates.' I could see her visibly soften as I painted our future in words around her.

'I suppose.' She replied reluctantly. 'What about mum though?'

'I think she will be joining us.' I said, hoping my uncertainty about it did not show on my face.

'This is a lot to take in Luke. I mean, I like the thought of being free and not worrying, you know like we were before the *gift*.' Her voice faltered to a whisper, and I wanted to scoop her up and wrap her in bulletproof cotton wool. I have never met anyone who was such a mixture of sass and vulnerability.

'I know babe,' I said soothingly, 'But our life can be pretty amazing there, and think of Chadd, and maybe his future brother or sister, picture them splashing in a pool and playing in a garden in the sunshine while we pop another shrimp on the barbie.' I winked at her, and she smiled, and I knew that she was won over.

The reality is we both knew that we had no option so there was little point fighting it.

SEVEN

Dani

I tossed and turned all night going over and over the words that Luke has said. Australia... it sounded so distant, almost as if it were another planet. It was a huge commitment and there would be no coming back if we left, and it felt, well it felt so final. I stared into the darkness and tried to coax my mind into feeling positive. We had moved to Thailand so we could relocate again.

I got out of bed as quietly as I could and went into the bathroom to freshen up. I looked at myself in the mirror as I half-heartedly attempted to do something with my hair and I wondered who I was sometimes, the never-ending trauma constantly numbing me, dangling happiness in front of me like an incentive, only for it to get snatched away.

I brushed my teeth and pulled on yesterday's shorts and vest top that lay on the floor and I checked on Luke and Chadd, who were still sleeping soundly. I let myself out of the room and made my way to the beach.

I loved being awake at this time in the morning just before the sun rose in the sky, when the planet spoke in sounds.

There was only one man out this early, a worker, raking the sand near the bar where the old men liked to play boules. He nodded but did not speak.

I could hear the waves gently folding onto the damp sand as I walked towards the steps that would lead me to the place where my soul belonged. It was like a silent calling from within whenever I felt unsettled.

I sat until the sun rose in the sky and the waves no longer kissed my feet and I stood, making my way back to my family. I had spent the past hour thinking about the positive aspects of the move and there were many things to feel excited about. I had given myself a stern talking to and decided that we would grasp this opportunity with both hands and make the most of our new adventure.

Luke woke as I entered the room.

'Are you okay? Could you not sleep?' he asked, as he sat up in the bed, brows furrowed in concern, his perfect lips pressed together anxiously. I underestimated how much Luke worried about me.

'I'm very good.' I said cheerily, as I smiled at him. 'I've been on the beach, thinking about our move and I'm excited Luke. I think it will be the best thing for us all.'

The look on his face tells me that this was not what he expected to hear.

'You serious Dani?' He probed.

'Yep. Maybe you could call mum and sort out what happens next with your job.'

Luke shook his head. 'You never fail to surprise me babe. Go and get the computer and we can look together while Chadd is still sleeping.'

We both agreed that Queensland would be the better place for us to live because of the weather and when we broke the news to Elanor she was elated.

'That's the best news I've heard this year and it means that Master Chadd can run around in a garden, and do the things that young children do, when he grows a little of course.' She added with a laugh. And so we had a toast to our future, a future that was feeling a little like Pandora's box; we would not know what it held until we opened the door to our new life.

Two weeks later Luke wheeled the suitcases outside while we waited on the taxi.

I checked the room for the fifth time and hurried around to the reception area where Elanor was patiently waiting with Chadd. I handed our key in to the lady at reception and thanked her for our stay in Koh Samui.

We had one night in Singapore together as a family before Luke flew to Australia, then Elanor, Chadd and I, would stay in Singapore for five days. Elanor was coming would be with us for the first three months, but then she would have to leave. I couldn't even begin to think about that, so I closed it off in my mind and compartmentalized it until I had to face it. At this stage Luke had no idea if he would even be eligible to be sponsored, it was all good and well Peter offering, but that was not a guarentee that he would be granted a visa and there was nothing we could do but wait and hope that it all worked out.

Luke stood with his passport in hand, case by his side. He has said goodbye to Chadd who had not got a clue what was happening. Lucky him!

'Dani.' Luke's voice broke through the layers of my detachment. 'How you feeling?'

'Fine.' I muttered, avoiding eye contact.

He walked up behind me and placed his hands on my shoulders, gently needing as he soothed me with his words.

'You and Elanor can plan some things to do with Chadd before you leave. You can visit the botanical gardens and visit the butterfly farm and the night zoo. He'd love that.' He said, far to enthusiastically.

'Yeah, I suppose.' I replied nonchalantly, and I was conscious that I was being passive-aggressive, making him feel bad for leaving me. I knew he couldn't help it, but I didn't know how I would sleep without him in the bed next to me.

'Don't look at me like that Dani please, I feel bad enough leaving you as it is.' He opened his arms and I melted into them, feeling his warmth flood through me, temporarily silencing the terror at being left without him in a foreign country.

'It's just that...' He silenced me with a kiss.

'See you in Australia Dani where we will all be safe.'

I think I saw a tear in his eye as he turned his back on me and walked out of the door, and despite his reassurances, I can't help but wonder if I am ever going to see him again.

EIGHT

Luke

After eight hours the plane touched down in Brisbane and sunlight flooded through the windows, while reflections from jewellery danced around the cabin like thousands of orbs.

As I walked slowly down the steps and onto the tarmac, I smiled to myself. I felt safe, and that was something that you could not put a price on.

I made my way through customs, which took the obligatory hour or so and then I walked through the departure gates and into a throng of people. A guy that looked like he belonged in Texas was standing with a board, my name emblazed across. He was tall and thin, and he was wearing some sort of cowboy hat that was not much wider that the moustache that adorned his face. His jeans were faded, and his boots well worn, a little like his face that cracked into a thousand wrinkles when I introduced myself. He was a walking advert on why to wear sunscreen.

'Luke G'day and welcome to Australia. The name's Mike.' He grabbed my hand roughly shaking it before turning to walk out of the exit. 'How was the flight?' He asked.

'Good thanks, got no sleep but that's standard for me on a plane. Do we have far to drive?'

'About a six hours' he said without flinching.

'Six hours, wow that's...'

'Don't tell me,' He interrupted, 'That's too far.' He let out a belly laugh and then shook his head before quietly saying to himself, 'You poms are something else'.

I followed him to his car and we pulled out of the airport and into the thick of the traffic.

'Is it really a six-hour drive?' I asked, and he laughed as if he'd been waiting for the question.

'It sure is and it's something that you'll get used to in time. It's a big country Luke, and sometimes it's easier to drive than fly, in any case you'll be doing it for a living soon so this will give you a chance to see some of the landscape on the way to Rocky.'

Right now, all I could see was a bustling city and a lot of traffic, it reminded me of home, only with sunshine.

Slowly the landscape changed as we drove further north. We passed road signs for wild horses and koalas, and even though it was only mid-September and early spring, the temperature gage showed it was 30c.

'Is it usually this hot?'

'Pretty normal for this time of year I'd say, it starts to heat back up around now before it cranks up for summer. If you can survive your first summer here, you'll be right.' He smiled.

I put my head back, suddenly overcome with the heat and the hours of travel. I close my eyes where Dani haunts my dreams.

I dream that we are on the beach and Chadd is older, maybe three or four. Dani and I are sitting on a picnic blanket watching him build a sandcastle. He carves out channels around his castle where the water will flow. A standard Mott and bailey. Chadd requests buckets of water to fill the moat that surrounds his castle and regardless of how we try to explain that the water will just sink into the sand, he still insists that he needs more water, so Dani and I take it in turns to run back and forward topping up his bucket. Suddenly there are screams in the distance and panic fills the air around us as wild horses gallop down the beach trampling over anything that gets in their way. Dani is running back from the water's edge, and I'm torn between staying with Chadd and running to get her. The horses get closer, and the sound of their hooves is deafening, and it is impossible to make out how many of them there are as sand flies up as they move across land at lightning speed, creating a sand storm around them. I wake with a start, surprised to find that I have been sleeping for almost two hours; that still left three hours to go.

Mike was playing country and western songs on his radio and singing along to them as I looked out of the window at the mostly flat landscape, dotted occasionally with a few houses and signposts. The closer we get to Rockhampton, the dustier it seems to get and the drier the land looks.

Once at the house I stepped out of the car and searched the horizon for a neighbour, but I was met with a wall of dense trees that surrounded the property. I'm not sure if this is a good or a bad thing. I estimate that I am standing on approximately five acres of land as I look toward the house and large wooden veranda that silently beckons me towards it.

The house was more modern that I had expected. There was a large kitchen-diner, a separate lounge room, utility, and three bedrooms, one with ensuite. There was split cycle aircon which Mike assured me we would need in the winter, and try as I might, I could not picture myself shivering with cold and needing to put heating on in this country.

The back of the house looked onto more land that contained a large double bay shed, and a small granny flat. The flat was self-contained with double bedroom, bathroom, and a small, combined kitchen and lounge; perfect for Elanor or Eva.

Mike told me that he lived on a farm a few kilometres from the property, but he looked after this land from time to time when the house was empty.

The nearest town was about a twenty-minute drive so there was plenty on the doorstop for our essential needs, and Brisbane was close enough to visit if we wanted a change of scenery. I was trying to sell it to myself because I knew I would have to sell it to Dani.

I thanked Mike, watched him drive off and then I called the hotel that Dani was staying in and asked be transferred to her room. She picked up after a few seconds.

'Luke, how is it? How are you? What is Australia like?' Her words all gushed out at once like an over-boiling pot. I wanted to tell her that it was too hot, too dusty, and that I worried about how Chadd would cope with the heat, but I didn't.

'It's great babe; you will love it here. The house is clean and tidy, and roomy, and there's a separate granny flat for El. We could buy a pool for Chadd and Brisbane is close enough to drive to for days out.' I didn't tell her it was six hours away because I wanted to paint a picture of safety, sunshine, happiness, and family days, everything that Dani craved.

'It sounds really nice. I miss you.' The desperation in her voice caused my stomach to tense.

'I know babe, but you will be here soon and then we will finally be able to live our life. The life we have always dreamed of.

I contacted my new boss who was based in New South Wales, and we talked through my role as supervisor of the new expansion. He seemed a bit pissed that a pom had taken a job rather than an Aussie, but he knew that I had connections to Peter, so he assumed it was a case of who you know, not what you know. I would do the deliveries myself initially, but my aim would be to build up the business in Central Queensland and employ others to drive as orders increased. I was free to choose my working hours as long as I met forty hours a week. That meant I could start at five am and I could be finished early afternoon, which would leave me time to spend with Dani and Chadd. I was already loving the balance between work and family life, and I hadn't even started work.

The next few days were spent getting to know the area and doing basics such as registering at a doctor's and setting up an Australian bank account. I prepped for the family's arrival by stocking up on new toys for Chadd, including a family outdoor pool with sun canopy. I picked up a few candles for Dani and laughed to myself imagining my mates from home seeing me now. I bought fresh bedding, towels, and enough food to last us at least two weeks and then I waited for my family to arrive, and I prayed that Dani would sail through customs. They were intense and had grilled me about why I was in the country and how long I intended to stay. I stuck to my story of travelling for a year on my work holiday visa, the rest would right itself after I got settled and became an employee of Peter's company. I had decided not to share my airport experience with Dani because I knew that she would work herself up into a frenzy and that would make her more of a target. She was due to land in three days' time at four pm and I had booked us into a hotel in Brisbane. The last thing she needed was a drive to Rockhampton after an eight-hour flight with a baby; and I wanted to show her what was available in the city before we made our way to our secluded property. I wanted to see what was available because only three days in I was already feeling as if I was living in the middle of nowhere. It was so different to Thailand and what we had been used to. For one, in Thailand we lived on the beachfront, and it was like being on holiday all year round. The waves rhythmically lulled you to sleep at night and then welcomed you to open your eyes in the morning. Dusty dry land just did not have the same appeal, and having no neighbours was a double-edged sword, and I wasn't sure how Dani was going to feel about that.

NINE

Dani

After an eight hour flight, we arrived in Brisbane on time. I almost cried when I saw the queue to get through customs. Chadd was wriggling in my arms and grizzling after the long flight and my stomach did a somersault when I saw the uniformed staff patrolling the area beyond.

'You're visiting on holiday?' The border contol officer queried when we eventually made it to the counter. His face was blank and expressionless. His eyes penetrating.

I nodded.

'How long do you plan on staying?'

'Eight weeks.' I replied nervously, and as quick as a flash he stamped the passport.

'Welcome to Australia'. He said, keeping his face in a fixed position.

We walked through the barrier toward the luggage carousel, and I sat Chadd in a trolley while grabbed our cases.

'I always feel like a criminal when I go through those check points.' Elanor said.

Try being a real one, I thought to myself. 'Let's get out of here.'

I wheeled the trolley towards yet another queue as I edged towards the immigration officers and hoped that they would not see my heart hammering in my chest. After checking my documents, I was waved through to the exit.

'Dani!' I heard a voice shout, and I looked around, Luke was pushing through the small crowd towards us.

He scooped Chadd up and kissed him all over his face, sending Chadd into squeals of laughter.

'I can't believe you are here babe,' Luke said excitedly. 'I've booked us into a hotel on Queen Street for two days. Tomorrow we're taking Chadd to Australia Zoo and I'm hoping El can look after him tomorrow night so that we can have a meal?' He questioned, throwing Elanor his best smile.

I sat in Luke's car and I closed my eyes, breathing out the tension that I'd been holding on to. I hear car engines, occassional horns tooting and planes coming in to land, as we drive away from the airport.

'Why is it so dark already Luke?'

'It's weird, isn't it? Apparently, it's because Australia is closer to the equator.'

Luke always knew things like that.

We parked underground in the hotel car park and took the lift up to reception. Once we'd changed Chadd and fed him we walked out onto Queen Street. I was amazed at the volume of people and the vast array of shops. There were souvenir shops, department stores, shopping centres, luggage shops, and clothes shops lined up either side. There were three stand-alone bars and restaurants in the middle of the pedestrian walkway; people sat sipping wine as they watched the hustle and bustle from their seats, while music played in the background.

'I love it Luke.' I gushed excitedly. Luke smiled but said nothing.

We spent a little time looking around before going into the food court to get something to eat, and then we went back to the hotel for an early night. It had been a long day for everyone, especially Chadd.

The following morning, we sat on the balcony looking across the Brisbane river at the traffic thickening, making its way into the city. I breathed in the Brisbane air, which had a distinct smell. An aroma of eucalyptus and coffee. The sun was already climbing the sky making me feel excited for the day ahead.

'Do you want to go to the zoo after breakfast?' Luke asked Chadd, who flashed a gummy grin even though he had no idea what a zoo was.

Later that night we left Chadd fast asleep in the care of Elanor and we walked down the street in search of food.

'There's such a mixture of people around. City workers dressed in expensive clothes, people in casual clothes, and lots of tourists with cameras. It's like there's a buzz of electric in the air.' I said as I looked around me smiling.

Luke guides us into one of the open bar/restaurants and we take a seat and scan the menu.

'I'm ordering steak because apparently the steaks are the *best in the world*. Luke said, with a grin that melted my heart. 'It's so good to have you here Dan, I've missed you so much.'

'Well, we are here now babe and I think we will be happy here.'

Luke smiled and distracted me with conversations he had with Mike.

'Queensland is lovely and there's so much for Chadd, especially when he grows a little older.'

'About that Dani,' Luke hesitated, and he looked nervous.

'What? What is it?' I asked sharply. I knew that look and it usually meant bad news.

'Initially I thought staying in the city was a good idea because it would show you what Queensland has to offer, but now I'm not so sure.'

'Why? It's great here. I like it.'

'I know you like it here and that's the problem.'

A young woman placed our food on the table. 'Enjoy.' She said, with a smile.

'Whatever it is Luke, let me eat first because this looks and smells divine; you can tell me after.' He opened his mouth as if to protest and I started cutting my steak up in a bid to stop him.

'That was delicious and now that we've found a good place to eat we can come back again,' I smiled, and Luke did that guilty look thing again. I make eye contact and raise my eyebrows, silently prompting him get whatever it is off his chest.

'The thing is, the house we're going to be living in is fine, it's just that it's in the middle of nowhere and I'm not sure that you're going to love Australia quite as much once you see where we live.'

'When you say in the middle of nowhere what does that look like exactly because I'm picturing lots of sand and no houses around.'

Luke shifted uncomfortably in his seat and took a big gulp of beer. 'Replace the sand with dirt and dust and you're just about there.'

'OK, give it to me, ' I said, 'How isolated is it exactly?

'Nearest neighbour is over two k's away,' He said quickly.

'Fuck.' I said, louder than intended and someone at the table next to us turned to steal a glance.

'I know it sounds bad,' Luke said hurriedly, 'But think about how much safer Chadd is in this country. How much safer we are. No one will ever be able to find us babe.'

'I guess we don't have a lot of options really. We'll just have to make the most of it.'

TEN

Dani

Two Years Later

We had planned a splash party at the local pool for Chadd's third birthday, so we rose early and watched him open his presents and then I raced to the pool and strung balloons up at one of the undercover seating areas. Life was so simple here and parties were none of the hassle I imagined they would be back home. If you had an Esky full of burgers, sausages, salad, and cake, it was fine. We cooked the food up on the free barbeques and the kids and parents played in the pool until they were hungry. Chadd had an amazing time and it filled me with such happiness to be able to see him surrounded by his Kindy friends.

Chadd had an amazing day with his friends. I stroked his hair as he lay in bed, the faint smell of chlorine still clung to him. 'Happy birthday, little Prince.' I whispered, as I kissed him goodnight. I would never tire of seeing him sleeping, peaceful, and happy.

The following day I grabbed the mail from the postbox and then jumped in the car, thankful for aircon. I had learnt soon after moving here to turn my car on at least three minutes before sitting in it, otherwise you risked melting into the seats and getting third degree burns from touching the steering wheel.

I turned up the music and opened the letter and smiled from the inside out. Life was good. I pulled the car into the car park at Kindy and waved to Julie, one of the other mums.

'Hi. How are you?' She asked as I stepped out of the car.

'I'm good Julie and I'm so sorry I didn't get back to you about the girls' night out, Chadd was unwell with a fever, and I forgot to text.'

'Don't worry about it,' she smiled and waved her hand as if to say it wasn't important. 'We'll catch up soon.'

The kindy door opened and parents streamed in as little ones raced for school bags and lunch boxes, little mouths all talking at a hundred miles an hour. 'Bye Rebecca,' Julie yelled over the noise as she tried to manhandle a pile of paintings from today's adventures, as well as toddlers. I smiled to myself and not for the first time I wondered if now would be a good time to bring baby number two into our lives.

I looked around wondering where my little soldier had got to, no doubt the toilet, which seemed to be flavour of the month wherever we went right now.

'Rebecca,' Kody, one of the child-care workers shouted and waved from behind a wall of children. I looked at her smiling young face and waved back. 'Chadd's already left.'

'Oh, did Luke pick him up?' Why would he not tell me? Wait until I got home, bloody driving all the way here for nothing, stupid arse.

'No, his uncle got him earlier, we did ring to confirm but you didn't pick up, but then we got a text from you seconds later so assumed it was fine.'

I felt the breath leave my body as I whispered, 'He doesn't have an uncle.'

'Are you alright, Rebecca?' Kody asked, concerned.

'It's a weird question but what did his uncle look like?' Blood pulsed in my ears.

She looked confused. 'Was he not supposed to take him?'

'No, it's not that it's just...' I didn't know what to say, and I thought I was going to vomit.

'He had a bald head, that's all I remember really.'

I ran out and she followed, shouting after me to ask if everything was okay. I turned the ignition on hit accelerate, far harder than I normally did and I was thankful that no kiddies were running around in this car park right now. I started shaking violently, sobbing like a baby. I reached into my handbag for my phone to call Luke and it wasn't there. My phone was missing.

I pulled the car over and opened the door just in time to vomit everywhere. I rinsed my mouth with water and shoved a piece of chewing gum in before mentally scanning my day so far.

I had only popped into the shopping centre to get a few basics and I'd always had my bag with me. My mind was going crazy, and the name Pez was jumping out at me continually, but I wanted to believe that there was some other explanation, a mistake of some kind, because the alternative I could not even bear to think about.

I raced home and was surprised I'd not been stopped by police, but I pulled up at home and I saw Luke's car and I breathed a sigh of relief. He was supposed to be at work for at least another three hours so he must have Chadd. Thank fuck for that! I had just turned the car off when Luke came running out, and I knew as soon as I looked at him my worst fears and nightmares had come true. We both frantically spoke at the same time. **Have you got him?** The words echoed in the air before I sunk to my knees and screamed. I screamed until the birds in the trees shouted back to me in confusion. Luke clung to me sobbing, both of us rendered speechless by the realisation of what had happened. My mind had turned to alphabet spaghetti, jumbled, senseless letters floating in a soup of despair, waiting for my brain to form a word. I couldn't breathe as blackness closed in around me. Fear saturating every part of my core.

I woke, confused, wondering if I had been dreaming, and then terror hit me again in a wave that sent me reeling. I clung to the bedcover for stability as dizziness sent me riding a wave.

'Luke!' I yelled in a croaky voice, having made myself hoarse earlier with screaming. He walked in eyes swollen from crying. The sickness that consumed me was like nothing I'd known.

'Oh my God. My baby is with that evil bastard. Luke what are we going to do? Please tell me!'

'Babe I, I just don't know what to do. If I go to the police then I have to tell them everything, and that means I end up in jail, as could you, because we will have to come clean about the name change and then we lose everything, we will be deported back to the UK where he can come and knock on our door any time of day or night.' He breaks into a sob. 'For fuck sake Dani I don't know what to do.'

'THIS IS OUR SON FOR FUCK'S SAKE! We have to call the police; we just won't tell them anything about the past or who we think it is. At least that way they'll be looking for him.'

'Of course. You're right. Sorry I'm not thinking straight. I'll ring them now.'

I could hear Luke on the phone talking out a jumble of words, not making a whole lot of sense to the person on the other end of the phone. I lay my head down on the pillow and Chadd's scent filled my nostrils and I thought back to only this morning when he had snuggled up next to me as he'd sneaked into our room just after six am, paw patrol pj's on and his favourite rabbit tucked under his arm. Panic swelled inside of me like vomit. I needed a drink. Elanor was inconsolable and part of me wanted to tell her to stop wailing, even though I knew that was really unfair, but it was just another sickening reminder that my boy was gone, and my mind was already crazy with possibilities.

I lay wrapped in my own despair until the police arrived.

Officers were talking into radios and mobiles and a man walked around the property taking photographs of everything. I watched out of the window, reluctant to be a part of it.

'Dani!' Luke shouted to me, 'The police want to speak to you, come on.' Luke urged, impatiently.

Several hours later, police had put together a description of the man that they suspect took Chadd.

An officer handed us a picture, Luke and I stared at the image, and I did an intake of breath, as memories of Pez come crashing back into my mind and body. I gasp for breath and hold on to the chair as the panic attack pulses through me with such intensity, I think I might die.

'Rebecca are you okay?' The officer asked, looking confused. 'You know this man?' It seemed more of a statement than a question.

Luke comforted me and tried to take over.

'I've never seen him before, have you Rebecca?' Elanor walked in with a glass of iced water for me and I took a gulp to steady my erratic heartbeat.

'No,' I stutter. 'I've never seen him before.'

'You reacted quite badly, are you sure you don't know him?' The officer asked, suspicion evident in his voice.

'No, no I don't. Sorry he just looks so scary and the thought of him having my baby...' I broke again, sobbing as pain ripped through me.

'Of, course, I'm sorry, we have to ask these things. Rest assured we will do everything we can to bring your little boy back. I know you will have been asked this question before, but have you had a fall out with anyone?'

'For fuck's sake,' Luke says, and I can see he's getting pissed off.

'Luke,' I whispered, and I looked at him pleading for him to calm down.

'We've not argued with anyone, I don't owe any money and I'm as far as I know, no one has a grudge against us, so instead of sitting here acting like I am some kind of suspect can you just get the fuck out there and find my son!'

'I need to lie down.' I walked out of the room without a backward glance and into my bedroom. I couldn't stand the lies, the pretending. The horror of this fucking situation. I rummaged in the bedside cabinet until I found the strip of Valium tablets, safely wrapped in their silver bubble coat; I popped two into my mouth and waited for the fog to hit my brain and send me to the land of no worries.

ELEVEN

Dani

Days had passed and nothing had happened. The police had appealed to the public for information and there had been a flurry of phone calls but nothing leading to Chadd.

I was terrified that the whole story would unfold; yet part of me wanted it too. Luke couldn't sleep for fear of the same, plus the added worry that he would end up in prison. I'd contemplated coming clean to the police, but the reality was that if I did that, I uncovered a whole lot of other people too, and there's no way Pez would hand my baby back when he risked losing everything, so all we could do was sit and wait it out.

Mum arrived and rather than make me feel better she made me feel worse. She meant well, but I simply couldn't cope with her following me around the house. Every single one of us felt helpless; we were living in this toxic bubble of lies, fully aware who was behind Chadd's disappearance but unable to speak up for fear of, well, fear of everything really. Our lives would be over. It was too much, and my mind was crashing in on itself, I could hear the demon voices calling me back to my old ways and each day they became stronger and stronger. The head chatter never stopped. I retreated into myself and spent more and more time in my bedroom, and less time communicating.

I wasn't sure what it was that Pez wanted, other than revenge. He had money, plenty of money, so this was about taking what was most precious to us, our darling little boy, and that broke my heart. All the past memories that I thought I had buried came back, stabbing me in the heart and making me wonder what he would do to Chadd. I cried myself to sleep numerous times a day exhausted due to the emotional stress and inability to sleep. I was lucky if I slept an hour each time and even then, the sleep was filled with nightmares about our baby screaming for us. I dreamt regularly that Chadd was trapped in a white building that looked similar to a lighthouse, only there were no stairs, just a spiral ramp that went up and up forever. I saw Chadd distressed, crying and running up the white-washed ramp surrounded by white washed walls. He ran crying for us, and nothing changed. He never seemed to get any further; he just kept running as if on a conveyor belt that was stuck, looking around shouting our names and crying, his little face distorted in anxiety. *Mummy where are you? Please mummy, don't hide. Daddy, please daddy.* I would wake gasping for breath, sobbing and clawing at myself to try and rip the pain from my insides.

A few days later the police told us that they had received information about a possible sighting in New South Wales. For the first time since Chadd had been taken, I felt hope. We all waited by the phone, watching some of it unfold on the local news where they showed clips of police vans and officers in white suits combing the area. Locals keen for face time on television jumped at the chance to speak into the microphone, while offering condolences; speaking of their shock that *something like this* was happening in their neighbourhood.

Eventually we received a call to say that the lead had turned out to be a hoax. All hope quashed in a split second, the dream of a car pulling up with my boy inside and us running to hold him, gone just like that! I walked into my room and closed the door. Mum followed at my heels, and I slammed the door on her face. I opened the patio door of my bedroom and I walked out of the house and through the trees to avoid being seen. I ordered a taxi to pick me up at the bottom of the drive and I asked to be dropped near the shopping centre, and then I walked until

I found the nearest bar and I ordered a whisky on the rocks. My mouth salivated as I watched the barmaid slosh it into the glass in what felt like slow motion. I observed the colour as it rolled over the ice, and my heart raced in anticipation of the taste. My mind had already closed off the rational voice that would normally have made an appearance, leaving no room for consideration of my consequences. My hand reached for the glass, shaking slightly with excitement as I tipped it to my mouth, savouring the smell before the liquid gold touched my lips. I rolled the nectar around my mouth enjoying the burning sensation, my tongue rough with appreciation flicked over my teeth, enjoying every drop. Oh God it tasted *so* good!

I ordered a beer and sat at a wooden table, chipped, and stained with years of wear and tear, and I wondered what stories this table would tell if it had a voice. I look at my mobile, put it on silent and placed it face down.

I ordered another whiskey, and then another, until the young girl behind the bar looked at me rather awkwardly before telling me that she could not serve me anymore. I felt like making a fuss, but I didn't have the energy and I suddenly felt really tired. The voice that was silenced had managed to find a way through the closed door, and now guilt overwhelmed me, and I started to cry, uncontrollable racking sobs. The young girl behind the bar was clearly out of her depth, looking around fervently for someone else to step in.

'You okay? Can I call you a cab?' She queried, awkwardly, as the tears kept flowing. A short time later a taxi pulled up, and the young girl tried to help me into it. I heard the driver launch into a speech about fees for vomiting in his car. He needn't have worried because the moment I gave him the address and lay back, I fell asleep.

The door opened letting in a blast of sticky heat and I could hear Luke's voice.

'For fuck's sake you've had me going out of my mind. Christ as if I haven't got enough to think of. How much do I owe you mate?' He asked the driver.

'Twenty-five.' I hear the driver say.

They exchange talk about where he picked me up from and whether I was alone. I can't be bothered to open my eyes, but I feel Luke carry me and lay me on a bed before ranting to Elanor and mum about something, and then I slip back into a land of blackness.

I woke to someone cracking my head open with a pick. My tongue was rough and my mouth dry, I sat up and winced in pain as my head pounded so I lay back down quickly. I pieced together the taxi, entering the bar and the glasses of whiskey; and my pulse quickened as it sank in how quickly my sobriety had come undone. I tried to recall getting home and drew a total blank. I felt sick now, not just with the raging hangover, but with the wonder at what I might have said, or done.

A gentle knock on the door snapped me out of my thoughts before Elanor opened the door, tentatively.

'You're awake.' She seemed relieved.

'El what time did I get home and was I a mess? Is Luke angry with me?'

'It was around seven honey. Do you think you can face food?' I noted that she had avoided the question about Luke.

'Toast please and coffee. Is Luke around?' She nodded. 'Ask him to come in please would you.'

'Would you like a bottle of water and two paracetamols as well?' She asked.

I smiled; she truly was an angel in disguise.

I closed my eyes wishing the next twenty-four hours away but also feeling the invisible string pulling me back towards the bottles that were lined up in the bar, just waiting for people like me to empty them. *People like me* - I roll that thought around my fuzzy head and I picture myself hanging off the bar laughing with people, my alter ego, drunk Dani; Dani that escapes real life through a bottle. Luke jolted me back to the here and now when he breezed into the room.

'Don't ever fucking do that again,' he said firmly, before grabbing me in his arms and hugging me so tight I thought I might throw up.

'I'm sorry.' I whispered.

'Promise me you won't do it again. Promise me Dani.' I look at him, desperate, hurting and I burst into tears.

'I felt so helpless, I *feel* so helpless. My brain, it hurts so bad because it keeps wanting to tell me what *he* could be doing to Chadd and every night, every single night and day, I dream of his perfect little face, and his gorgeous smile, and I see him in my dreams crying for us and I know in real life he will be so *so* confused and terrified. I just wanted to block it all out Luke. I just want the thoughts, and the pain, and the fear to go away. I just want our baby back.' He pulled me too him and lets me cry it out while rubbing my back like you would a child.

'I know baby,' he soothed. 'We will get him back don't you worry. We will.'

I desperately wanted to believe him, but the skeptical side of me that had seen how people like Pez worked, doubted every word Luke said.

TWELVE

Dani

The alcohol monster had helped me build a transparent bubble. I could see people from within the bubble, but I couldn't *really* see them. I could *hear* people, but their words bounced off. I felt as if I was trying to communicate through a fog that I could not penetrate.

I saw Luke's face and I could make out his features, worry etched in lines he never used to have, weariness and frustration evident. He shook me once when I had stood there in front him with a drink in my hand, he shook me and then he hugged me and apologized over and over. He begged me in a faraway voice, begged me to stop the drinking and take control of my life again, and some days I wanted to, I really did; and other days I surrendered to the monster and appeased it with the liquid that it needed to survive, and so the monster grew stronger each day, as my resolve grew weaker.

One day I left the house when Luke went out and Elanor was hanging washing. I knew that Luke had told El to keep an eye on me because I heard him as I lay on the bed riding the wave of dizziness that pulsed through me. I took my car and I drove to town and parked the car in a car park off the main street so it would be less likely to be spotted. I walked in to the nearest bar, not caring about anything other than ordering a drink. I bought a bottle of cider and a double whisky and sat at a table near the back of the pub.

I was feeling good about being out of the house and not so good about everything else that was happening, so I downed a few drinks relieved that I did not have Luke, mum, or Elanor, chewing my ear. I walked over to the pool table and put some money on, so that I could play the winner. It had been so long since I had done anything like this, since I had just hung loose, got drunk and had a laugh. I swallowed the rest of the whisky and smiled to myself. My goal today would be to get so drunk I would forget to remember that my son was missing.

'You okay love?' A man asked as I almost lost my footing on my way back from the bar.

'Why wouldn't I be?' I fired at him in annoyance, but the words came out of my mouth in slow motion, and it did not have the impact I had intended it to have.

'Easy tiger,' he said with a half-smile. 'Just checking that's all.'

'Sorry. Yep, I'm fine.' I say, knocking back my drink.

And before I know it I'm playing pool and a few more men have joined us and we're all drinking together.

'Not bad for a Sheila.' One of them said.

'Who the fuck is this Sheila anyway?' I asked, and they all roared with laughter. I know I'm drunk because it's the only time I swear and I should probably go home now, but I'm having a laugh and forgetting things I don't want to remember, so I go to the bar to order another drink.

'I'll get that Julie.' A dark-haired guy says.

'My name's not Julie, I said, confused.

'Aren't all you pommies called Julie?' he asked, and I realize he's taking the piss out of me.

'Funny aren't ya.' I said, as I grab the drink and walk off. I raise it in the air.

'Cheers for the drink Bruce.' I see two of them wink at each other in a suggestive way and it fires me up.

'Whatcha winkin at?' I slur and I try to maintain my balance, simultaneously.

'Nothin darling.' He replied, before whispering to his friend. They laugh.

Those fuckers are laughing at me. My mind starts travelling backwards to when Pez used to laugh at me as I lay on a bed, in the shower, or on the floor begging him to stop, and I could feel a rage building inside of me. I walked over, well weaved a little, but I stood in front of the winker, and I pushed him.

'Think you got it all wrapped up don't you, Bruce?'

'Woah what's going on?' A voice from the bar area shouts.

'Someone stop Sheila's drinks, she's turnin all psycho on us.' They sniggered.

'Fuck you!' I screamed. 'Fuck you all. You haven't a clue.' I staggered towards the door, chest heaving with humiliation and desperation, and one of the quieter ones followed me outside.

'Hey, are you okay?' he asked, and I slumped to the floor and sat against the wall, overcome with alcohol and pain. I felt as if I was about to tell him my story but then a car pulled up and Luke jumped out.

'Jesus Christ, I'm going to have to keep you under lock and key.' Luke pulled me up and I fell against him, slurring the words sorry.

'Hey, do you know him?' The stranger asked me.

'Mate, if I was you, I'd take your beer and piss off back into that pub. Of course she knows me, she's my wife.' He shrugged and walked off as Luke tried to manoeuvre my clumsy drunken body into the car.

'You are going back to Thailand to rehab. I can't keep doing this Dani. It's unfair and it's fucking selfish of you. I'm hurting too and I don't need this shit every few days when you piss off on a bender.'

'It's been four weeks Luke. FOUR WEEKS! They haven't found him.' I slur and sob. 'He's dead I know it.' Drunk Dani is not afraid to share her deepest fears or secrets.

Luke grabbed my shoulders. 'Stop talking like that! Chadd is not dead! You've already given up; what the hell is wrong with you?'

I wake hours later on top of my bed, still groggy from the alcohol.

'I can't deal with my anxiety and alcohol is the only thing that takes it away.' I look at Luke, hoping he understands.

'We've been through this vicious cycle before, remember. You wake, and you have too much adrenalin flooding your system from the alcohol, so you think *oh I know I'll go and get pissed to take it away.*'

I knew he was right. I needed to get a grip for my son's sake; I should be out there looking for him not trawling bars picking fights with strangers.

'OK, I'll do whatever, I'll go to AA, I'll see a doctor, but no rehab, I need to be here for Chadd. I want to do something though, Luke. I hate the sitting and waiting because the day and night merges into endless empty hours and it's driving me crazy.'

'I know how you feel but what can we do?'

'We could come clean.' I test the water, saying it quietly.

'Tell the police everything? There's no way we could uncover his whole operation without huge consequences.'

I already knew this, but I was feeling desperate.

'What's the alternative Luke? He's not going to hand Chadd back to us.'

'He won't want to attempt to leave the country with a kid, especially when he doesn't have a passport for him.'

I nod silently. *Dear God,* I say in my head, *Please return our son to us unharmed.*

Thirteen

Luke

I sat up in bed and watched Dani breathing lightly in her sleep, shuddering now and then as if an unpleasant thought had shaken her to the core.

She drove me crazy. There was no getting through to her when she went AWOL. I call it that because it feels like she is missing even when she is here. She retreats to a place when she is scared and hurting, and she automatically builds a wall around herself and shuts everyone else out. There's no predicting when she will take off to find refuge in a bottle and that pisses me off. I know her past is the main reason, but it is like dealing with a wayward teenager when she is in that headspace. Dani had done so well since Chadd had been born but this was too much for her. Too much for me. I was struggling to stay positive but knew that I needed too, but it was hard. The police were suspicious. They kept saying that there should have been a ransom note by now, and it made me nervous. All it would take would be one officer and one question, a drunk Dani, and she was likely to spill her heart out. Some days I prayed she would do it, to take the responsibility of what to do next away from my shoulders. I closed my eyes and tried to force myself to sleep, desperate for a break from the worry.

At five am my phone vibrated on the bedside table next to me. I opened my eyes confused for a moment as I wondered who would need to call me at this time of the morning. I slide out of bed trying not to wake Dani and answer the phone.

'Hello.'

'Luke. It's Sargent Tully, we have Chadd at the hospital. He's fine, a little disorientated and dehydrated, but we think he's relatively unharmed. He's not allowed to be released until a doctor has given him a full check over though so you and Rebecca might want to come to the hospital.'

I sank to my knees and silently thanked God about a thousand times and then I ran into the room.

'Dani wake up, they've found Chadd,' I shouted.

Dani sat bolt upright in the bed and started hyperventilating.

'It's fine babe, he's okay, a little dehydrated but other than that the doctor thinks he's doing good. Get dressed and we can go and see him now.'

Dani went into autopilot dressing herself, but she remained silent.

'Hey are you okay?' I asked her as I turned her towards me. Silent tears were coursing down her face, and she was shaking like a leaf. 'What is it babe? I thought you'd be ecstatic.'

'I am,' she hiccupped, 'it's just that, well, what if he doesn't know who we are anymore?'

'Of course, he'll know who we are.'

'You're right,' she said, wiping her eyes with the back of her hand. Her breathing was fast and uneven, and I sensed her anxiety was getting the better of her.

'We need to move Luke.' She said, and I sighed and rubbed my face, already exhausted with the conversation we were about to have.

'I know how you feel because I feel the same; but we can't babe. We cannot keep running. We have gone from the UK to Thailand, and now to Australia, and he's still found us. Moving somewhere else is not going to stop him.'

'Why are you saying that? Fucking hell Luke, my anxiety is at an all-time high and now you start throwing shit like that around.'

I got up and pulled her to me, but she resisted.

'Sorry. I'm just so strung out with it all Dani. I seriously don't know what to do next. I can't sleep at night, and I'm scared to go to work in case I come home and you're gone.' She looked at me shocked, like a deer caught in the headlights.

'Helpful!' She turned her head and pulled a face that indicated I had been anything but.

'Look Dani, the more I think about this the more I think I should just come clean to police.'

'We've lied to them through this whole thing. I mean, I know I said tell them everything but we have Chadd back, so why now?' Dani asked.

'Because I am over running away from it all.'

She stormed off and I followed her.

'Don't you dare go AWOL on me.'

She spun around with a look of disgust on her face and opened her mouth to say something, but nothing came out. I'd hurt her. 'Low blow, Luke.' She said, lips quivering but stubbornness stopped the tears from flowing.

'I didn't mean to upset you, but it's what you do Dani, you run when things get too much, and to be honest I can't keep holding everything together, at least not all of the time, sometimes I would like you to be there for me instead of going off into your own world.'

She put her head down and her shoulders started heaving as the tears poured out of her like little drops of poison.

'Look we need to figure something out when we get back from the hospital, but for now let's try and keep it together for Chadd's sake. Let's focus on getting him home and once he settles down we can talk about what to do next. It won't be good for him moving again, especially not now.' I said.

She nodded, and we sat silently as we drove to the hopsital in hope that we could bring our son home. *Home.* I rolled the word around my mouth like a marble. I didn't know what home meant anymore. We had moved around so much and every time we got settled, we were up and off again. Home no longer offered safety behind closed doors; in fact it was starting to feel like a prison cell with no doors. I wondered how I would ever be able to sleep. I questioned how many times over the years Pez had sat outside of our *home,* watching us go about daily life. I was beyond thankful that my son had been returned, but I couldn't help but wonder what came next.

I knew deep down that I had to return home and confess everything to the police, the question was, would Dani come with me? Without her I had a half-baked story that held no real evidence, other than my word. With Dani on board, they could put Pez away, but we had Chadd to think of as well ourselves. It was a conversation we needed to have, sooner rather than later, but right now my priority was making sure my son was OK.

FOURTEEN

Dani

We arrived at the hospital and as we step out of the lift an officer escorts us to Chadd's room. The sweet smell of fear hung in the air.

There is a strange woman sitting on the cot bed next to my son. There are metal bars around the side of the bed as if to stop him falling out, but one side has been dropped and the woman is sitting close to him, observing his every move. He's playing with a small wooden puzzle, but he seems distant and my heart lurches in my chest. I rushed forward, all of my worry and stress momentarily disappearing as the longing to hold my boy in my arms takes over. The woman moved quickly from the bed to block me, she stepped in front of me confidently, as if she had the power to override me as parent. I instantly disliked her. She has shiny blond wavy hair that sat half-way up her neck. She's wearing blue dress trousers that are far too baggy on her small frame and a fitted cream shirt. She smells expensive. I tried to move sideways, but she moved with me like my shadow. What the fuck was her problem?

'Rebecca,' she smiled, and reached out a hand to shake mine, reluctantly I obliged.

'Marsha', she said. Stupid name, I think, and I stare at her trying to figure out what her role is and why she thinks it's okay to stop me connecting with my son.

'Excuse me,' I said tersely, 'I would like to see my son.'

'Chadd's been through a lot.' *No shit Sherlock!* 'It's best not to overwhelm him, so if I was you, I would take it easy. He's still traumatised.'

'Yeah,' I say defiantly, 'I think I know my own child thanks very much and I'd appreciate it if you moved out of my way.'

She put her hands up as if surrendering but there was a know it all look on her face.

'Chadd, baby,' I said as I bent down to him. 'It's mummy.'

'Mummy' he said as he wrapped his arms around my neck, albeit loosely. He let go far quicker than I would have liked. I sat next to him and asked him questions about what he was playing with, he looked the other way and ignored me and I felt a stab in my heart. I turned to Luke who was chatting to Marsha.

'Luke.' He stopped talking and made his way next to me. I felt a small victory over that woman, and I had no idea why I had launched myself into an invisible competition with her.

Luke tried talking to Chadd. Chadd lifted his head and looked at Luke, only it felt as if he was looking through him not at him. He turned away and continued to repeat his pattern of play.

'Marsha said that it's normal for him to respond this way after what he's been through. She said he will still be processing everything.' Luke parroted, sympathetically.

'What does she know?' I snapped. 'What even is her job title anyway?'

Luke stared at me in a way that told me he did not approve of my bitchiness.

'She's a child psychologist, I think she knows her job and she is trying to help.'

I swallowed the lump down that was rapidly growing in my throat.

'I'm going to get a drink.' I said and left the room. I ran into the bathroom and cried and then I rung mum.

'Mum it's me,' I sobbed. 'Chadd won't even look at me. I'm sure he blames me for letting that man take him from school.'

Mum soothed me and coaxed me into going back into the room and as soon as I walked in I saw that damn woman playing some kind of cat and mouse game using just her hand. Chadd giggled and it momentarily made me smile. At least he still knew how to laugh.

'Can I have a word, Rebecca?' Marsha asked.

'Sure,' I said, and I knew I sounded aloof. I could not get a grip of what was wrong with me.

'Look I know this is hard, I understand how you're feeling.'

'Do you?' I interrupted. 'How do you know what I'm feeling? Have you ever had a child of yours abducted before? Infact do you even have any children?'

I saw her close her eyes long enough to tell me that she was trying to restrain herself from responding to my rudeness. She ploughed on as if I had not spoken.

'I'm here to help support you Rebecca, if you are ready. The way Chadd is responding is perfectly normal. Everything in his world has been turned upside down, the people he loves and trusted disappeared and because Chadd is so young, you may never know the extent of what really happened when he was not in your care. All tests indicate that he has not come to any physical harm, however the psychological impact of being ripped away from his family will take time to heal.'

I felt a stab in my heart because I knew how it felt.

'I don't know how to help him.' I said, ending my imaginary feud with her.

'Just be there Rebecca, that's all he wants; normality is what he needs.'

A female officer called Luke and I out of the room. She beckoned us into a small room that was empty and smelled of sad news. I pictured relatives hanging off each other crying as they were drip-fed the reality of losing a loved one.

'Luke, Rebecca, sorry to take you away from your son, I just wanted to update you about where things are at. A farmer spotted a young boy fitting Chadd's description crying as he was bundled out of a car and into a shed. By the time police arrived Chadd was alone in the shed and obviously very distraught.'

I started to cry, huge racking sobs as I thought about my baby lying there all alone wondering where we were.

'Oh my God, my poor little boy. How is he ever going to recover from this and how do we protect him now?'

'It will take time and the child psych can help you through the worst of it. In regard to who took Chadd, we're still looking for them. Forensics have scanned the whole area but so far, we have very little to go on, apart from the description of the man that collected Chadd from Kindy.' A pause. 'And you still feel that you do not know the man?' She questioned in a way that implied she thought we knew more, or maybe that was my guilt superseding everything.

'As we've already said, about a thousand times, we do not know him. What I want to know is what do we do now? What if this maniac comes back and tries to take him again? Or worse!'

'I understand your concern and we have already flagged your address on the police system, so if any calls come in, your address becomes priority. We have also worked closely with the kindergarten that Chadd attends and I know they have completely reviewed their policy around allowing other people to take children from the centre. We can have someone install cameras outside of the property and apart from that I guess all you can do is ensure that your house of safe. Keep windows and doors locked at all times, and maybe buy a dog?'

None of that helped ease my anxiety. I should have been feeling relief that Chadd was safe, but instead I felt an all-consuming fear about him being taken again.

I walked back into the ward with Luke and the doctor was checking Chadd over. It was uncomfortable to watch as Chadd squirmed and rejected the doctor attempting to take his temperature.

'Can I speak to you both please? I just need to run through some basics with you about Chadd's aftercare. We have done basic bloods, temperature and x-rays and so far, all that has shown up is that Chadd was dehydrated, and obviously traumatised. You will probably find that he will suffer from night terrors, but that's to be expected. His brain is not developed enough for him to process everything that he has been through. I would advise you to link in with your normal GP who will be able to monitor him and make any necessary referrals in order to further support him.'

'Is there anything else we can do?' I asked, desperation soaking my voice.

'Unfortunately, we cannot predict how Chadd will respond once home, so it will be a case of one day at a time. Trauma affects children differently, but the brain has the capacity to heal itself so try not to worry too much, and never underestimate the resilience of children.'

As I made my way towards his bed, I looked at my baby boy through the bars of the cot; there was a moment when we made eye contact and I felt as if I was looking into his soul, he was confused and hurting and I needed to stay strong for him to help him through it.

FIFTEEN

Dani

We drove home with Chadd strapped into his car seat and suddenly I felt nervous about being a parent. I was terrified of saying or doing the wrong thing and I felt unsure how to comfort my child. In many ways I felt like a child myself and I longed for someone else to take charge and tell me what it was I needed to do. I hated the second-guessing and 'taking each day' as it came because that meant uncertainty, and I struggled with the vagueness of that. Chadd remained silent mostly, only speaking when he wanted a drink or food, but he clung to me like a second layer of skin, terrified of being taken away again.

That night when he was finally asleep, I walked into the lounge, leaving the door open so I could hear him if he stirred.

'Luke, I think we should take him to a child therapist. I've been it checking out and play therapy allows children to express what they've been through, using play rather than words.'

'If you think it will help babe of course we'll do it.'

'God knows what happened when he was in that shed, he could have been shut in there alone in the dark all night.'

The phone rang in the kitchen and I rushed to answer it before it woke Chadd.

'Hi mum how are you?' I asked. Mum had left two days ago, after I begged her to go home. I thought it was just too much for Chadd having so many people watching his every move. She was upset at first, but she understood that he needed time to recover.

'I'm good darling, how are you and my beautiful grandson, and Luke of course?'

'We're OK mum, Chadd's sleeping. Have you recovered from your jetlag yet?'

'Hell no, I was up at three am. I'll be no use to anyone by early evening. In other news, Peter has bought a beautiful house in Wales. Despite only being in Spain a short time he missed home, and obviously it's not safe to go back to our hometown so we opted for a change of scene. Abersoch will be our home a few months of the year. It's a little seaside village with a small population and Peter has a cousin that lives there.'

'I wish I could visit to see what it looks like,' I said, as a feeling of nostalgia washed over me.

'I know darling; I wish you could come and visit too honey.' I hear sadness in her voice, thick like syrup and it knocks the air out of me.

I have to admit, I'm relieved that your house sold.'

'Exactly darling, it's a fresh start.'

I smiled as I thought about how far our relationship had grown over the past three years; it was one of the few good things to come out of the horror.

'Come and play, Chadd.' He looked at me and did not move from the sofa, glued to a children's cartoon. I'm not even sure he was watching it, he was transfixed to the screen but seemed zoned out. 'Come and help me build a castle with your building blocks buddy.' He shook his head and gripped his comfort blanket tighter. I stood up to leave the room to make myself a coffee and he made a whining sound, almost like a half-hearted cry.

'No.' He demanded loudly.

'No what, Chadd?' I asked quietly.

'Stay here.'

'It's okay, I'm only going into the kitchen to make coffee baby. You can come if you want.' I turned away, stomach churning with anxiety. The therapist had suggested that we stop feeding Chadd's fear by acting as we had prior to the abduction; apparently it would help recondition his brain in time. The more we pandered to him the worse his anxiety would become. I wasn't sure it sounded right but I was lost in dealing with this, so I trusted that the therapist knew what she was doing.

Chadd followed behind me angry, crying, and running at me. He gripped my legs tightly and then nipped with his fingers.

'No Chadd, it's not okay to do that.' I felt awful telling him off, but I also felt frustrated dealing with his changed behaviour. I felt like I was walking amongst a minefield every day, uncertain what would set him off or when he would blow. The triggers changed daily so it was hard to anticipate what the right thing to do was.

I kneeled and looked him in the eye. 'We're going to get you dressed and we're going to the swimming pool. Mummy loves you.' He looked back and then lay his head in the crook of my neck and sucked his thumb.

Ten weeks later the therapist reported that Chadd was making good progress, and more importantly Luke and I were noticing change in him. We saw more glimpses of the fun, active little boy we were used to. Night-time was still place of horror for him, and I for one could very much relate to that, but, he was making progress and that was all we could ask for.

I dropped Chadd off at Kindy, reluctantly, knowing that I was doing the right thing trying to keep his day as normal as it could be. I hated leaving and had to force myself out of the door and into my car. The drive home was always a pain staking one, with thoughts of returning to collect him and him not being there. I knew they would never let anyone take him again, but the fear never left me.

I made myself a coffee and waited for Luke to get out of the shower.

'Do you fancy going for a drive today, or a walk maybe?' Luke asked, as he entered the room. 'I thought we could go to the botanical gardens and have lunch. I'm sure Elanor would be in her element if you asked her to bake a quiche. You know she likes to be busy.'

'Sounds nice,' I said, lying. I hated that normal day activities fuelled a rage inside of me. I found it difficult to visualise myself sitting eating a picnic as if my life was normal when it was far from it. I was reminded daily when I walked into a shop to buy a newspaper, or food. I saw the nudges and heard the whispers. There were kind people who asked how Chadd was out of genuine concern, and then there were those that were just plain fucking nosy.

'I'll go and ask Elanor if she fancies baking and then I'll do an hour's work. I'll be back here for twelve.' Luke said. I nodded and made a half- hearted sound to pretend I was interested. Luke left for work and I sat in front of my computer scrolling through Facebook as if I had nothing else to do.

Elanor was already busy baking a chocolate cake for Chadd, and she was now starting on sausage rolls, quiche and jam tarts. I couldn't help think that Luke's idea had been a good one if only to save me cooking dinner later.

Blaze our new guard dog, a very serious looking rotwieller, bellowed out a series of threatening deep barks and I looked at Elanor, nervous as to what had set him off. Several minutes later a florist van pulled up and a woman got out, rummaged around in the back of the van and then brought out the biggest bouquet of flowers I have ever seen. She stood next to her van waiting on someone going outside.

'Sorry I'm not risking my life for some flowers,' she nodded towards the dog.

'I get you, I'm not exactly best friends with him either but I have to say he definitely does his job well.'

'Thank god for that chain,' she laughed. 'He might have ate the van and me in it otherwise.'

I thanked her and then placed the flowers on the kitchen table. I threw a bone outside for the dog.

'Good boy.' He looked at me briefly before taking his meaty reward in his jaws, slobbering all over the ground.

I remove the card from the envelope and read the words.

My mind tumbled down a familiar dark tunnel. Elanor touched my shoulder, and I screamed in fright as I pulled myself back from the depths of despair.

Elanor read the card and colour drained from her face as if she was leaking blood. 'Call Luke.'

'I will as soon as I've called the Kindy.' I say. My heart is racing and hands are shaking so hard I can barely hit the numbers on the screen.

They reassured me that Chadd was safe and well and I slumped into a chair and cried out my overwhelming anxiety.

'This can't go on Dani. Something needs to change. I'm not sure what, but this is ridiculous, we're all living on a knife's edge.' Elanor said.

I swallowed, my throat tight and constricted, air filtering through in thin shallow bursts. I dialled Luke's number.

'What's up babe?'

'A huge bouquet just got delivered. The card says *I'm watching you.*'

Silence.

'I'm leaving work now.'

'Are you okay?' Eli asked, and I stayed silent because I had no words to describe how I was feeling right now. 'I know that's a stupid question, it's just I don't know what else to say Dani.'

'I'm not sure there is anything left to say. This has gone on long enough, you're right.'

I waited at the window for Luke to arrive and my mind was already zoning out, retreating to a place of emptiness with nothing but blackness; presently, I favoured that over reality.

Luke pulled up and got out of the van, anger spread taut across his face as he grabbed the mail that was sticking out of the mailbox and marched towards the house. The dog seemed aware of his mood and did not make the usual barking fuss but stood up and observed him before lying back down in the shade, escaping the saturating heat of the day.

Luke hugged me and then picked up the card, before letting it drop from his fingers as if it had burnt his skin.

'Fuck! I have had enough of this. I'm flying to England and I'm going to the police Dani. I don't care if I get sent down, as long as he gets put behind bars and this stops!' Luke shouted.

'I can't lose you. I wouldn't be able to cope with all of this without you.' I sobbed. Our eyes fixed on each other, but there is silence sandwiched between us. Why was he not reassuring me? 'Say something Luke.'

'We need to talk Dani.' He walked into the lounge and I followed him, numb with fear about what lay ahead.

Sixteen

Luke

My temperature reached boiling point by the time I arrived home. I told Dani I was going back to England to sort this once and for all. I see her eyes widen and adrenalin kick in, her pupils were dilated and her skin almost translucent, which bizarrely made her look like one of those china dolls; all pale beauty and eyes.

'I can't do this anymore Dani, so please don't beg. It's something I've been thinking about for a while and believe me I am aware of the implications, and I know you will struggle with me doing this, but you have to admit that we're kind of backed into a corner.' I looked at her. 'Say something. Please.' Silence. Now it was my turn to wait. 'Dani!' She blinked and then seemed to be with me again, almost as if a switch had been flicked.

'I'm not sure what to say to you Luke, I mean, you're signing your own death sentence doing that.'

'I know that, but I am prepared to risk my life if this stops for you and Chadd.'

Her face changed and the old feisty Dani entered the room.

'Oh, please, save the fucking heroics Luke. I don't need to hear that shit; I want you here with me!'

I see her in fight or flight mode and know that I will have to keep a close eye on her.

'I'm not being a hero; I'm putting an end to this. Or do you just plan to let him continue with this until our number is up?'

She sat on the sofa head in hands, breathing heavily. I knelt next to her but refrained from touching her.

'Dani look at me,' I urged gently, as you would to a small child. She raised her head slowly, and I saw the pain in her eyes.

'I know you're right Luke, that's why I am fighting this. I know we have no other option, but that doesn't stop me being terrified. I can't stay here without you. I don't even feel safe with you here, never mind if you're on the other side of the world.'

'I get that you're angry, and scared, Dani, but I'm going to go insane soon, because every waking minute of every day I worry I will come home to an empty house and a message written in blood, or that I will be pulled from my bed at night and tortured before I am killed. I'm worried that Chadd will be taken again and not returned. I can't sleep and I can't eat properly because I am so consumed with the on-going game of threats. Sometimes I think it would be easier if Pez just came and killed me, because at least it would be over. I no sooner want to do this than I want to throw myself into a lion's den, babe.'

'So how will it work, Luke? Where will me and Chadd go and how will we stay safe? And what about Elanor?'

'I can't answer all of that right now. I think the first thing we should do is let your mum know that I plan to do this and hopefully she can put me in touch with a good solicitor, then I will explore what to do next.'

'Wow that's reassuring,' she said, as she walked out of the room without looking back. I followed her like an obedient puppy to see where she was going.

'I'm taking a bath, Luke, so fuck off following me.' Despite her venomous tongue I couldn't hep but laugh, and I was grateful that she was not a sobbing mess right now, anger was good because that meant she was focused and hopefully after she had processed everything she would calm down.

I kept out of Dani's way for an hour then made her some food and walked into the lounge.

'Peace offering?' She gave me a look that told me she was no longer mad at me.

'I'll call mum when it turns six, she'll be up by then, and it looks like she needn't bother booking another flight here.'

'Tell me that we're are on the same side here, Dani.'

'Yes and no; I understand why you want to do this, and part of me just wants this whole thing to be over as well. I just want to live a normal life instead of feeling as if we are on the run, but I'm terrified of one or both of us ending up in prison.'

'It won't come to that,' I said with false bravado. Dani raised a perfectly sculpted eyebrow.

'You a lawyer now?'

'Sure, and I sentence you to an afternoon in bed, naked.' She laughed, and I felt as if we were a team again, and that just strengthened my belief that I was making the right decision.

Seventeen

Dani

I braced myself for the conversation I was about to have. I knew how worried my mum would be when I told her Luke's plan.

'Mum, hi, how are you?'

'I'm fine darling, but you don't sound it, in fact, you sound rather flat, what's up?'

'Oh God mum it's been an awful day -.'

There was silence and I imagined mum trying to process what I'd just said to her.

'What are you going to do?' Mum, asked.

'It's not so much what I'm going to do, it's what Luke's going to do. He's had it mum, there's no going back now.'

'What on earth do you mean there's no going back? What's he done Dani?'

'He's going back home,' I say, and a sob escapes and tears start flowing.

'Why? Why would he do that?' Hysteria is evident in her voice.

'He said he's going to go to the police and telling them everything, he wants to put an end to this once and for all.'

'What about you and Chadd, and Elanor? You can't stay there on your own!'

'I know. I haven't even had a chance to think about where we will go because he just dropped the bombshell today and he's not changed his mind. If anything, he is more determined than ever that he is doing this.'

'But Dani,' She paused as if reluctant to say the next words. 'In order to tell the police everything that means Luke has to bring you into it. He can't go making decisions like that on a whim!"

'To be fair mum, it's hardly on a whim. I mean our son was kidnapped and now I'm receiving death bouquets from the fucking psycho.'

'I would give anything for this to be over for the three of you, but I just can't see how going to police will make this go away darling, and that terrifies me.'

I end the call and close my eyes, warding off the demon inside that pushes me to escape this living hell. The smell of alcohol rising from my memory reminds me of what lies beyond the door. I resist, but I'm unsure how long I can fight it.

I've been thinking, Luke, and it's obvious that in order to nail Pez for his drugs and prostitution racket, I am going to have to agree to be a part of this.'

'Not necessarily.' He said, confidently.

'Luke, are you in denial or do you seriously think I am completely stupid? How the fuck can you expect police to charge him without a witness.'

'That's the thing, if I give the police his address in Wimslow then they will find the other girls and they will have their evidence.'

'That *could* work, but how do you link him to the drugs? I guess what I'm saying is that no matter what, he has to go down for life if you go to the police, because we can't risk a ten-year sentence and him getting out in three years to start over again. Have you thought about when you plan to do this? We need to agree on some sort of plan about when you go, where Chadd and I go once you leave.'

'I don't know what to suggest Dani but you making me responsible for every-one is not helping. Why is it up to me to have all the answers?'

'Sorry. I know I'm pressuring you, I'm just scared.'

We sat in silence before agreeing to sleep on it, in the hope that daylight would bring some clarity, or a miracle!

The following morning, I rose early and sat on the wooden deck with a cup of chamomile tea listening to the kookaburras laughing loudly, waking the other birds up, which caused a cacophony of noise. The sound felt familiar now, and despite my growing love of this dry and dusty land, I knew what I had to do. As the sun rose I made my decision. After four years of running, I was going home.

Later that night Luke and I sat on the veranda, the smell of citronella circled around us warding off the mozzies, as the warm November air wrapped around the trees, prompting cicada's to sing their song.

'I sat here this morning,' I said to Luke. 'It was so strange. I listened to the kookaburras cackling in the trees and I watched the sun rise in the sky and it was almost like an epiphany.'

'What was?' Luke asked quizzically.

'I want to talk to the police. I want to tell them every detail I can remember and I want to be there when Pez gets locked up. I want to go home Luke. I've had enough of running.'

He reached for my hand. 'Are you sure?'

'Yes, I'm sure. I can't stand the thought of Chadd being taken again; we have to fight back.'

'I agree. We can't change our mind once we make that commitment.'

I nodded resolutely.

'I'm not going to tell mum the date we are going back, I think we should just surprise her.'

Luke turned to look at me. 'Christ Dani, she'll have a heart attack.'

'Don't be stupid. She'll love it, and it means she won't have time to stress about everything. It's actually a good thing.'

'And Elanor? Are you just going to send her back to Spain again?'

'Don't say it like that Luke, as if we don't care about her.'

'Sorry, it's just a bit overwhelming thinking about it all.'

'It is, but in a strange way I also feel liberated. It's like a strength has emerged within me and that overrides all of the *what ifs.*'

'What do we do with all of Chadd's toys?' Luke asked.

'Donate them to a refuge. We can buy him some more, it's almost Christmas anyway.'

'I'm worried. You seem too calm, and I'm not sure if that's a good or bad thing.' Luke said.

'Would you rather I was sat here sobbing? Or worse, had ran off to the pub?'

'You know I wouldn't, it's just that I'm used to the stressy Dani. You make it all sound rather straight forward but it's not.'

'I know this isn't going to be easy and I am fully aware that there will be fall out, but as you have said many times over, we are already suffering every day. At least this way we stand a small chance of being freed from all of this.'

'If you're sure but maybe think about calling your mum first.'

'Everything will be fine Luke and mum will be thrilled to see us.'

I slept well that night, dreaming of a gilded birdcage with a door slightly ajar, offering freedom. It was close enough to see, but too far away to reach, but it gave me hope that eventually, one day, we would be able to open that door and taste the safety and freedom that we all deserved.

EIGHTEEN

Dani

Outside of the airport I hugged Elanor as she sobbed and spoke in Spanish, dabbing at her eyes.

'*Mi hermosa niña, mantenerse a salvo*,' my beautiful child stay safe, she said, as she made her way toward departures. It felt like saying goodbye to my best friend and mother all rolled into one.

'It's for the best Dani. She will be safe with her family in Spain.' Luke said, and I nodded. Words stuck in my throat as I choked on my silent heart break. I was fully aware that I may never see her again, so I waited at the airport until her plane had climbed into the sky and I walked back to the car, wearing acceptance like a weighted overcoat.

The following day, Luke, Chadd, and I boarded a flight to Edinburgh. I breathed a sigh of relief when Chadd fell asleep, his head on my knee, his feet on Luke's.

'I think I made the wrong choice not telling mum.' I said to Luke.

'She'll be fine. She'll love seeing Chadd.'

'But will she really? Us being at her house puts her in a vulnerable position. Again.'

'We didn't have any other choice. My mum can't help in any way, it will be fine, stop stressing. We'll have a lovely couple of days in Edinburgh, we'll be able to show Chadd the Christmas markets and take him to see Santa. He will love it, babe.'

I nodded and closed my eyes and let fatigue sweep me into the darkness.

We arrived in Edinburgh at six-thirty pm on the first of December. The air was so cold it knocked the breath out of me and made me cough. We took a cab to the hotel, taking in the volume of traffic and lights shining through the darkness, and once in the room all three of us crashed out and slept until five am.

'I don't want to wear a hat with a ball on top,' Chadd stated, stubbornly. Luke and I burst out laughing.

'Darling, you have to, it's freezing outside and you are used to being in warm countries. Scotland is very cold and it's winter now. If you don't wear this, we can't go to see the rides and go and see Santa.'

Huffily he agreed, but I sensed that it would be a battle we might have several times over the coming days.

Stepping outside of the hotel was a sensory explosion. We were situated on Princess Street and lights were twinkling as far as the eye could see. Christmas Carols were pumping out of the market place that was decked out with trees, and a man dressed as Santa stood on the street corner ringing a bell and yelling "Ho Ho Ho". The smell of hot chocolate and cinnamon permeated the air.

'Look there's Santa!', Chadd yelled excitedly before escaping my hand that was loosely gripped around his mitten. He ran off in the direction of Santa.

'Hello young man what's your name?'

'Chadd,' he said, quietly but confidently.

'Chadd, it's nice to meet you.' Chadd looked at us with a huge smile on his face.

'I would like a bike Santa, and a remote trole car,' He said quickly.

'Well, I can't promise anything, but I will send a message to my elves and you never know, you might just get a lovely surprise on Christmas day.'

'Thank you, Santa,' I said with a smile, as I steered Chadd away from him. I felt warmth flood through me despite the cold that nipped at my flesh. It felt good to be back home. Simultaneously, the voice of fear crept into my happy head to remind me that my time was limited.

'Are you OK?' Luke asked.

'I'm fine,' I lied, as I swallowed down my fear like a bitter pill.

We spent the rest of the day exploring shops and markets and Chadd had a ball on the merry go round. He'd never seen anything like it before.

'Look mummy, I'm flying on a horse.' he said, his blue eyes were sparkling and his little nose was red with the cold. He looked so happy and months back I'd never imagined we could see this side of him again.

We spent our second day walking around Edinburgh Zoo, fighting jetlag and an icy wind that wrapped around you like barbed wire. Chadd absolutely loved it, and even though Luke and I were chilled to the bone, we watched his face light up whenever an animal made an appearance.

The following morning we picked up the hire car and set off at eight am for our six-hour drive to Abersoch in Wales. We stopped for lunch at a farm café and Luke and I ate while Chadd ran around with a bottle of milk attempting to feed goats; it was hilarious to watch and I was pleased that he seemed unaffected by the change of country.

As we got closer to mum's house the hills turned a deeper shade of green and in the distance, snow lay on top of the mountains; it was one of the most beautiful sights I had ever seen.

'Look Chadd, snow on the mountains.' I said, as he clapped his hands and started shouting for Santa.

'Oh God, what have we done?' Luke asked half laughing. 'Your mum's going to be insane by the time Christmas comes.'

I smiled but felt my stomach sink.

'I don't want to go to the *people* until after Christmas.' I said firmly. Luke furrowed his brow in confusion.

'What people mummy?' Chadd asked, and I saw it register with Luke.

'Fair enough,' he said, and I was thankful that we would get Christmas with our little prince before our life was turned upside down.

We drove into Abersoch and the smell of salt water and seaweed filled my nostrils while nerves danced in my stomach as we rounded the corner to mum and Peter's new abode. It looked like a house that the Famous Five could have grown up in, with a picket fence and lush green grass that invited you to sit on it with a picnic blanket, and a wicker basket full of food.

We walked up the path encouraging Chadd to be as quiet as possible.

'We're playing a trick on Grandma so when she opens the door you shout surprise, but you can't talk or giggle until she answers the door.'

'OK, Mummy,' he whispered, as he rushed up the path. I knocked on the door and after a few seconds the door swung open.

'Surprise' Chadd shouted and rushed at my mum. I looked at her face, a mixture of delight, confusion and fear swirling in her eyes, along with unanswered questions the probed me with an invisible finger.

'Sorry mum, it was my idea to surprise you. I realised when I was almost here it was a stupid idea, but it was too late by then.'

'But you just text me yesterday saying how hot it was.'

'Mmm, yeah, I lied. We were in Edinburgh.'

Her lips pursed in disproval.

'We went to the Zoo Marmar,' Chadd interrupted.

'Did you darling boy? You'll have to tell me all about it.' Mum said, as she led us into the house.

The house was so modern inside which was strange because from the outside I had pictured old-fashioned fires in the rooms, wood floors, and flowered wallpaper glued to the wall with secrets.

The entrance of the house was large with a staircase in the middle of the floor. Carved wooden horses with wild manes adorned the end of each handrail, the dark mahogany wood contrasting against the cream carpet. There was a large kitchen to the right of the entrance, a fair size dining room directly behind and a large lounge to the left with a library that faced the back of the property.

'Wow, nice house mum.'

'Isn't it. It's large enough for Peter and I.' She coughed, then looked at me awkwardly. 'I didn't mean...'

'It's fine,' I interrupted. 'I'm sorry that we turned up unannounced and we can easily book into a B&B, really we wouldn't mind.'

'Don't be silly, of course you can stay here, but we do need to talk darling.'

'I know. I'll take Chadd for a walk in a minute to burn some energy off, he's been sitting in a car all day.'

'Sounds like a good idea, and I had better call Peter and let him know that you are here. He's just at his cousin's house helping him with something.'

When Luke and I finally sat down with mum, and Peter I felt unbelievably nervous. The table was set with matching white floral dishes that were filled with mashed potatoes, an array of root vegetables and a large roast pork that was partially sliced. Luke bit down on some crackling and broke the silence.

'Well as nice as it is to see you three, a phone call wouldn't have gone a miss.' Peter said, clearly unimpressed with our surprise approach.

'I'm sorry Peter, that was all my idea and Luke was against it. I knew that if I told mum we were coming back she would start stressing, and I have put her through enough, I really wanted to minimise her stress and thought this was the best way of doing it.'

'Your intentions were good Dani, I can see that, however your mother is stressed now about what happens next.'

'I am capable of speaking for myself Peter, thank you,' Mum said gently, but firmly.

'Luke and I both agree the only option we have now is to go to the police together and tell them everything.' I said, sounding far braver than I felt.

'And Chadd?' Mum asked when she found her voice. I cleared my throat nervously.

'That's the part I need your help with.' I pushed the words out as if they had a bitter taste. I hated asking for mum's help again after everything she had done for us. I watched Peter's lips press together as if he was physically trying to stop himself from saying something.

'Your mum has been through enough Dani. You haven't seen her fall apart; you haven't had to pick the pieces up. And it's unfair to expect her to look after a young child of Chadd's age. This is ludicrous.'

'It's fine Peter.' Mum put her hand up as if to silence him. 'Dani, I will give you a number for a good barrister, he was a friend of your father's.'

'Thanks mum; and Peter I really am sorry for bringing this to your door.' I said, genuinely. Mum was silent and I wasn't sure how to read her thoughts about it all. 'I have money, I will pay for a nanny so mum doesn't have to do anything other than provide a roof over Chadd's head.'

'How long does this go on for Dani? One year? Ten years?' Peter demanded. 'And what about Australia? All of the strings I pulled to create a position for Luke under the pretence of expanding my business.'

'Yes I know, and we will both always be grateful to you for everything you have done. Surely you understand why we came back though. Chadd being taken was a step too far and then wreaths arriving for Dani consoling her on her loss!' Luke said. Peter looked at mum who turned as red as her lipstick.

'I think I forgot to tell Peter about some of that, we were so busy with the move and I didn't want to spoil our new start,' mum said, awkwardly. 'But I think we can all agree that the sooner this is over the better for us all.'

I woke early at four am and I shivered my way to the bathroom, touching the large metal radiator that was attached to the wall to check if it was on. I pulled a jumper out of my suitcase trying not to wake anyone and I eased my way down the stairs as quietly as I could. It was so cold I almost hugged the kettle as it boiled. It was black outside and rain ran quickly down the window as if trying to escape, and my stomach churned as I thought about our meeting with the barrister later today. I sipped my coffee and jumped as Luke walked into the kitchen.

'I almost had a heart attack,' I said.

'Stressing about today?'

'I guess.'

'It will be fine.' Luke said resolutely.

'Maybe,' I said, wishing I could summon some positivity from somewhere. Right now, I felt all out of hope that everything would turn out okay. My mood was as dark as the sky outside and there was absolutely no rainbow on the horizon. All I could think about was being away from Chadd, stepping into a Tardis, into the unknown.

After a short flight to London, Luke and I walked into Craig Simpson's office and took a seat in the waiting room. It felt more like a hotel lobby with its plush tartan chairs, chandelier, and marble floors.

'Daniella, Luke, you can go through to Mr Simpson's office, he's expecting you.' A model like PA said with a smile that was should have been promoted by a toothpaste company.

I walked nervously towards the door and knocked out of courtesy, waiting for a prompt to enter. The door opened surprising me, and a handsome man much younger than I had imagined greeted us and ushered us to seats.

'Sorry I didn't mean to scare you. Please come in.'

'Before we start would anyone like a drink?'

'Water please.' I wished it was vodka to numb my anxiety.

'I need you to tell me absolutely everything from start to finish. Do not miss anything out. Once we have done that, I will evaluate your options.' Craig said.

I found myself fumbling for words that had gone into hiding,

'My time is precious and expensive so I find the no mess approach best for you, the client, because it saves you money and I can quickly assess if I can work with you.' He said.

I took a deep breath and started talking and once the wall of silence had been broken, I found it hard to stop. Several times Craig took a break to digest what he had been told and more than once I saw the colour drain from him when I talked about being held hostage in the house. I told him everything I could remember, from the countless rapes to the beatings and humiliation. Luke also told him about his role in the drugs and about how he suspected Pez had killed Mick.

'Guys I need to sit on this overnight. There's so much information I really need to think through what will have the best outcome for both of you. Can I call you tomorrow?'

We left the building, and I watched people rushing past, cold wind biting them, making them retreat further inside of the coats that they were wearing. I noticed how their shopping bags weighed them down as they pushed on with their busy little lives, no time to lift their head and see the sky above them or make conversation with a stranger. Each person living in their own world, cut off from everyone around them. That's what life was like now, segregated into invisible walled communities; the rich who mingled with their own, the middle class who tried to mingle with the rich in hope some of it rubbed off on them, the normal families who worked all hours never to really see a benefit from it, and the ones the country had discarded. It made me realise how lucky we had been to live in Thailand. We woke to the sound of the ocean, we ate fresh food every day because there were no supermarkets selling pre-packaged meals. We lived a basic but fulfilling life that revolved around the things that mattered. We had everything that we had needed: a house, food, each other, our baby, and Elanor. I hadn't cared what the house we lived in looked like because inside was filled with love and happiness. In Thailand I had thought we could put the past behind us. I'd been wrong.

Nineteen

Luke

As soon as we walked into the building Craig was waiting for us with a nod and brief smile. It was hard to know this meeting would turn out, and my stomach was starting to chew over the breakfast I now wished I'd not eaten.

'Take a seat,' Craig gestured to the chairs in front of his desk. 'I have some good and bad news.'

I looked at Dani who was gripping the chair.

'I spoke to the Crown Prosecution Service this morning and given the extent of this whole operation; the drugs, the prostitution, kidnap, deprivation of liberty, money laundering and so on, the CPS is prepared to drop all charges provided you both agree to give evidence against this man.

Dani started crying. 'I thought that we were both going to prison. I'm so relieved.' She hiccupped.

'There's something you need to know before you start arranging the celebration party,' Craig said. He looked serious.

'The CPS only become involved in cases when the witness is at risk of harm, and when I say harm, I mean death.'

'We already know he wants to kill us Craig,' Dani said.

'To be part of the prosecution service you have to be prepared to say goodbye to your old life in every area.' He looked at me first and then Dani.

'That won't be a problem, we've already done it once and moved several times.'

Craig cleared his throat and shifted his shirt collar awkwardly as if he'd suddenly become too hot. 'This would be slightly different because it would mean cutting ties with all family in order to keep you both safe.'

'I only have my mum, and her partner, and Chadd of course. Luke's mum is in a nursing home.'

'When I say all contact, I mean your mum as well Dani. It would be a case of you, Luke, and your son moving, and not being able to see those family members again. You can't go and visit, you can't tell them where you live and you cannot under any circumstances post on any social media.'

I looked at Dani and saw the impact of Craig's words hit her as if they were physical objects.

'That's ridiculous!' she spat back at Craig before turning to me. 'Luke.' She looked at me as if wanting me to resolve the situation.

'You have to understand that it is the only way police can keep you safe. They can only protect people that agree to follow the very strict rules.'

'When would it happen?' I asked.

'If you decide to go ahead you have to sign paperwork and be prepared to provide evidence at a police station, and because this case is complex in the sense that there are two huge operations with drugs, plus trafficking and prostitution, the case could go on for years. Police will want to ensure they have enough evidence before they make any arrests. All of that takes time, so you need to know that this guy is not going to be locked up anytime soon. Hence the need for your protection.'

'Fucking hell! So, we put our whole life on hold indefinitely while police faff around gathering evidence?' I say.

'That's pretty much the bottom line, Luke, because without that evidence there is no case, he will get off. It will take more than your word against his.'

We sat in silence.

'Take a few days to think about it, there's a lot to consider.'

'If we decide to go ahead, what's the process? Dani asked, voice wavering.

'After you've given evidence you get a call and it will be a case of pack a suitcase because a car is on the way to collect you, you will have one hour or so, and then your life will change forever.'

'I can't wait to tell mum this!' Dani said, sarcastically.

'You would most likely be moved around if there was any suspicion that you were in danger. It's not a life for everyone, and often people decide against it because of the strict protocol you have to follow. Talk it through with your family and call me in a few days.'

I thanked Craig, even though I wanted to scream at him. I knew that he was only the messenger, and he was just doing his job, but I wondered for the umpteenth time why the fuck my life was so difficult.

TWENTY

Dani

As I opened the door to mum's house Chadd screamed my name and ran at me from the lounge.

'Mummy look, look at Santa tree.' My mum laughed as Chadd pulled me by the hand urgently towards the lounge where a Christmas tree stood in front of the window, lights twinkling. 'See Santa tree mummy?'

'It's a Christmas tree baby, not a Santa tree,' I said, as I scooped him in my arms and covered his face with kisses as he squirmed and laughed. He smelled like cotton candy. 'Has grandma been giving you treats?'

I watched Chadd for the rest of the day chatting with my mum and it broke my heart because I saw how much she loved him. She was nothing like the woman who I grew up with, the coldness had well and truly gone and she revelled in being around her grandson. I wondered how I could possibly break that news to her that she may never see him again.

'What are we going to do Luke?' I whispered.

'I think we both know what we HAVE to do Dani, but it won't be easy.'

'I don't even know how to tell mum that she will never see us again. It's so final.' The words taste sour in my mouth as I set them free.

Luke took my hand and squeezed it. There were no words that could reassure or comfort me.

After Chadd had brushed his teeth, I read him a story and watched him fall into a land of sleep. He looked like an angel with his long dark lashes lying against his creamy skin and I wondered how I ever got so lucky having this mini human in my life. I gently stood up, careful not to disturb him, and I walked downstairs, each step knotting my stomach tighter and tighter.

'Your mum has had a new lease of life since you came back Dani,' Peter said with a smile. 'I've never seen her so happy and it's quite special to see how she is with Chadd.'

Fucking hell, kill me right now! It was as if Peter knew we were about to pull the rug from under their feet. Guilt rendered me silent, but I managed a small smile.

'How did the meeting go? You've both been very quiet since you returned, and I wasn't going to ask any questions in front of the little man.' Mum smiled as the last two words left her mouth.

I looked at Luke as if trying to gain some invisible strength from him.

'In some respects, it went great, in others it was terrible.' I said.

'Tell me darling, I'm on tenderhooks here.' Confusion clouded her eyes.

'Well the good news is that if Luke and I agree to give evidence then there will not be any charges laid against us.' I said as brightly as I could considering the emotion that was strangling me.

'That's fabulous darling, but is it safe?' She asked, looking at both of us.

'That's the bad news mum.' I paused and closed my eyes. 'In order to keep us safe we would have to agree to go into the witness protection program and that means we have to cut all contact with everyone.'

'That's not difficult given that you did that when you moved to Thailand honey.' Mum smiled.

I visualized a ginormous needle about to burst her bubble. 'When I say everyone mum,' I turned away from her as tears filled my eyes.

'That includes you and Peter, Eva.' Luke said, solemnly.

'Don't be so ridiculous. Police can't expect you to do that!'

'They do and we have to sign paperwork to say we will live by those strict rules.' Luke said, gravely.

'So, they will move you somewhere and you're saying I can never see you or Chadd again? Is that what it will mean?' Mum's voice has risen, and she was on the verge of either having a melt down or erupting.

'Calm down love,' Peter said, as he attempted to rub her back in a comforting gesture. Mum spun around.

'Calm down. Calm down! How the hell do you expect me to do that?' Peter stepped back as if to keep out of it for fear of saying the wrong thing. 'I just can't get my head around this, Dani.' Mum said.

'How do you think we feel?' I looked at her as tears coursed down my face and my heart stuttered in my chest. 'It's awful mum. There just seems to be no end to the sacrifices we have to make. I can't imagine not seeing you again and Chadd asking about you. I won't be allowed to send photographs or keep in touch via social media either. Apparently, crims like Pez have a computer whizz to track people down, and once they can get into email accounts they find out all kinds of information about where you are living. We have to let Craig know by Friday which is only forty-eight hours away.'

'How long do you have to stay in the program for?' Mum asked in a whisper.

'Indefinitely.' I said before breaking down. Luke put his arm around me, absorbing the sight in front of him.

'That fucker has so much to answer to!' Luke said, before storming out of the room. I let him go because I knew there was nothing I could say.

'I'm sorry mum. I feel like this is all my fault and no matter how hard I try to put it behind us it just won't go away.'

Mum let out a sob and Peter moved to comfort her. I walked out of the room and into the kitchen to escape the grief that was burning in the room like a candle. It was snowing, just a few rogue flakes here and there, but it was one of those moments that transported me back to my childhood and Christmas time. Dad used to pull me around the garden on a wooden sledge that he had made for me. We would build a snowman if there was enough snow, before running into the house, hands numb and noses red. We would drink hot chocolate in front of the fire while mum wittered on about us being crazy for going outside in those temperatures. I was pleased that my dad was no longer alive, because this would have killed him.

I put my coat on and walked outside to find Luke. I turned the corner and saw him sitting on a seat looking out to the harbour. Icy wind whipped me as I made my way towards him, walking against the invisible wall of wind that was tempting me in a different direction. I watched the flakes of snow swirl around in the air like dancing fairies, before landing on the ground and dissolving into nothing more than a wet spot. Luke turned to me as I got nearer. Sadness sat in his eyes when he looked at me and I sensed his tiredness of living this life.

'Sorry,' he said looking at the ground, 'I needed to get out to clear my head.'

'If this icy air doesn't clear it nothing will,' I joked.

'Fuck Dani, I'm over this whole thing. I feel like all of a sudden, I'm struggling with all of it. The rage I feel inside is like nothing I've know before. I just want it all to end.'

'I know, Luke. ' I held his hand, grasping on to my anchor.

'I'm terrified of losing you both, but I can't stand the thought of living a life in hiding forever either. It just seems so unfair that Pez gets to do what he wants, yet we are always looking over our shoulder.'

I nodded because there was little else I could say.

We slowly made our way back to the house. From the outside that solid brick house looked like it was holding everything together, but I knew that inside it was all falling apart.

The next morning there was tension in the air and mum keeps looking at us. A few passive aggressive comments fell out of her mouth as she tried to emphasise how much Chadd loved spending time with his grandma. I knew it's a struggle for her and I said nothing because I was still processing everything myself.

My phone vibrated against the wooden table and Craig's number flashed up on my screen making my heart lurch in my chest. I wait until it stops ringing, and then look at Luke, neither of us want the responsibility of saying let's do this.

'I'll call him,' Luke said before walking upstairs. I heard muffled voices and felt my chest tighten, wondering how long I had left, before life as I knew it disappeared before my eyes.

Luke walked back down the stairs twenty minutes later with a holdall. Breath stuck in my throat like a solid mass.

'It's OK, we're not going anywhere yet babe.' Luke said. 'I spoke to Craig and explained we're not doing anything until after Christmas.'

'What's the bag for then?' I asked.

'I've decided to go and see my mum one last time,' he said, solemnly.

'Chadd and I will come.' I gushed, wanting to support him.

'No babe, I have to do this on my own. You understand, don't you?' His eyes pleaded with mine.

I didn't, but I nodded. Luke kissed me and squeezed me tight. 'Never forget how much I love you.' He said. And then he was gone.

TWENTY-ONE

Dani

For the rest of the day I wandered around from room to room like a lost soul. There was something wrong, I could feel it in the air around me. A knot of anxiety sat in my stomach. I called Luke but it went to voicemail, again. Maybe he's driving I said to myself to quell my fears, and it occurred to me that I had no address or contact number for Luke's mum. God, how crazy was that? I flicked back over the years. I had met Luke when we were young and only interested in partying, my mum was driving me crazy at that time so I never talked about my family at length, and I never asked Luke about his. Fast forward me being held hostage, and I realised it was one of those topics we had never discussed until I was pregnant with Chadd. Even then Luke had been vague, upset even, and when he said not to push him to talk because his mum was in a nursing home and had dementia, I respected that. I felt stupid now. I visualised walking into a police station to report him missing and saying the words, *we've been together five years, but I know nothing about his family and have no idea where his mum lives*. I felt heat rush to my face and dizziness wash over me.

'Are you alright? You're off in your own little world.' Mum asked, making me jump.

'Yeah, sorry, I need some air I think, I'm almost dead on my feet, bad night's sleep. Is it OK if I take a walk and leave Chadd with you?'

'Of course, he's happy playing with the train set that used to be around the Christmas Tree,' Mum laughed. I popped my head around the door and heard him talking to himself about Santa delivering presents to all of the good boys and girls.

I walked to the harbour and sat on the wall, tasting the salt air on my lips as small grains of dry sand danced around my feet whenever a gust blew. I watched the waves push forward sending slivers of water towards my feet, as if trying to reach out and grab me. Something big was coming, I just couldn't work out whether it was the witness protection thing, or something else.

I put my hand in my pocket and reached for my phone, realising that I'd left it in the house, so I walked back pushing against the wind that was now as fierce as my gnawing anxiety.

'I'm back,' I shouted out to the empty room.

'We're upstairs building a tent for Chadd,' Mum shouted.

'I'll be up in a minute,' I replied, my eye catching sight of the green flashing light on my phone. I tapped in my password and saw a missed call from Luke. I listened to the voicemail.

Hi babe, sorry I was driving. I'm here, and I want you to relax, everything is going to be fine and remember that I love you and Chadd. You're everything to me . Nausea swirled around my insides as I listened to the message again. I dialled Luke's number, but he didn't pick up, nor did he over the next twenty-four hours. I called Craig to see if he had heard from him and I told him that I was considering going to the police. He advised against it.

'There's something not right mum. I've had this feeling since the day he left. His decision to go and see his mum was so sudden.'

'Calm down honey, you're getting worked up for nothing.'

Two hours later I received a text message from Luke saying he would be staying another couple of days because his mum was unwell. *Tell me where you are, and I'll drive there.* I pleaded. He responded with another message that said he would be home before I knew it and it would all be over.

What was with the cryptic fucking messages and avoidance? I called again but as per the last five times it went straight to voicemail. That night I lay in bed knowing fine well sleep was hiding from me. I played everything over in my head since we had returned from London, looking for some kind of sign. The only thing that had been off was the phone call that Luke took upstairs, the call from Craig. He had come downstairs afterwards with his holdall and the notion to go visit his mum, which was just odd.

I woke at five forty-five and wrapped my dressing gown around me to keep the cold air out. I opened the curtains and sat on the sofa sipping a cup of peppermint tea, trying to ease the nausea that sat inside of me. It was still dark outside and bleak looking, which matched my mood. I wrapped my hands around the cup to warm myself, aware of the silence apart from the cracking of the radiators as they warmed to life.

I called Luke eight times that morning and each time it went to voicemail. The nausea grew.

Later that day I was sat watching television with my dinner on a tray, a meal that had been forced upon me by my mum who was worried because my appetite had all but disappeared, along with my partner it would seem. My mind was off in its own disastrous world where all endings were bad endings, when words from the television filtered through my brain, causing my heart to run a race no one else could see.

'... *approximately one hour ago in what appears to be a gangland shoot out. One of the suspects who has been identified as Peree Ezpinossa, is believed to have been one of London's most notorious drug dealers. Police have refused to release any further details at this stage; however reports are that there were several fatalities.*' There on the screen in front of me was a picture of flashing lights. I dropped my plate as vomit rushed into my mouth, forcing me to rush to the kitchen sink.

'Dani, what on earth is wrong?' My mum asked as she rushed after me.

The air I breathed felt as if it was void of oxygen, so I sucked in more and more until my head swam.

'Dani!' My mum shook me and forced me to look at her. 'Tell me what's happening!' She ordered. All I could do was cry and release the tension that had been building inside of me like a volcano. Mum waited until I composed myself.

'I knew when he left, I knew there was something wrong.' I hiccupped. 'I've felt it since he walked down the stairs and it's so unlike him to not call me.'

'You're not making sense honey.'

'The TV mum! The TV!', I shouted. Mum looked at the TV and then back at me, obviously unaware of the conversation that had just taken place. 'There's been a shootout in London and a man called Perree Esino or something like that, was shot.'

'Now I'm even more confused,' Mum stated.

'It has to be Pez mum. I think Luke might have just killed Pez.'

She pulled back from me as if I'd spoken with a forked tongue, a mixture of disbelief and horror rolled across her face like a dark cloud. 'Oh, come on now Dani, that's a bit of a long shot isn't it? Just because his name begins with the letter p doesn't mean it's the same guy you had dealings with.

'Had dealings with?' I spat at her.

'I didn't mean it to come out sounding like that, sorry darling.'

'It's him I know it and now I need to find out where Luke fits in all of this.'

I could see mum was torn between wanting to calm me and not wanting to encourage my hysteria and wild theory.

'How about I call some of the hospitals?' Mum suggested. 'Which area was the incident in?'

'Woodford, just outside of Wilmslow,' I said, and I see her eyes widen as if my crazy theory could be a possibility.

'Well let's hope someone has shot that vile man, preferably not Luke though,' She said firmly, before walking off with the phone in her hand.

'What is it? Is it Luke?' I asked when she walked back in. I was rooted to the spot, unable to move.

'Darling sit down, I want you to sit down.'

'That's what they say in the movies when they're about to give someone bad news mum, stop.' I said, robotically. Fear pulsed through my veins.

'There's no easy way of saying this but Luke is in hospital in intensive care.' The staff have passed on his next of kin details to the police, apparently, he had no wallet or anything on him so they had no idea who to contact. I think it's safe to say we can expect a visit from them some time soon, so I suggest you call Craig and get some advice about what you do or don't say at this stage.

I sat numb, frozen with terror that he might be taken from me. 'I can't lose him mum. What if the police want to speak to me before then? What do I say? Do I come clean and tell them everything or say nothing? Mum help me! I don't know what to say, I'm scared I could end up in trouble. And I need to see Luke!'

'Oh God Dani, I have no idea. Please call Craig now and take advice from him.'

I dial his number and it goes to voicemail. Fucking great!

'I've booked a flight for three hours and you're staying at a hotel not far from the hospital.' Mum said.

'You said *you're* not we're. Are you not coming with me?' I cried.

'It's no good me coming now and being cooped up in a small room with Chadd; a hospital is no place for him.'

'So I have to deal with this on my own?'

'Only for a few days honey and then I'll sort something. Go and pack Dani there's not time to hang around.'

I arrive at the hospital four hours later and I breathe in the antiseptic air that encases me as I walk through the door; I can't help but think that it's the smell of death.

I get pointed in the direction of the intensive care ward and my body forgets how to breathe. My legs feel heavy, reluctant to walk any further but I push through the doors of the ICU and into a corridor that seems to echo my heart-beat.

At first, I think it is deserted, but then I come upon a a nurse whe smiles at me, breathing life back into my shrinking lungs.

'Can I help?' She asks gently.

It's a perfectly logical question, but for some reason the words *I'm looking for my partner* refuse to leave my mouth.

'Are you looking for someone?' I nod.

'Male?' She queries. Again, I nod mutely. 'Can you give me a first name?'

'Luke,' I whisper. I see her register his name and then her expression changes.

'Come with me,' she says tenderly, and I follow her into a lounge room. My heart beats rapidly.

'Please, take a seat, my name is Astrid.' My first thought was that her name didn't match who she was; my mind started to drift as I thought of names better suited to the creamy complexion and shiny dark hair. Suzy maybe, or Carol; yes, she looked like a Carol, happy, caring, and all kinds of shiny. Memories of Astrid from the rehab took me back to another lifetime.

'Hello, do you have a name?' I jumped back into the present, embarrassed because Astrid had been talking to me for who knows how long.

'Sorry, my name is Dani,' I said, realising immediately that I had not used my alias of Rebecca. Astrid started talking and I caught words like poison darts.

Life support; critical; next twenty-four hours.

'What happened to him?' I asked as tears coursed down my face and my body shook spontaneously.

'He was shot several times. You need to prepare yourself before you see him, because he will look different.'

I nod but don't understand what she means.

'Would you like to see him now?'

I follow her silently to a room.

'Call if you need me. There are two of us here all of the time.' She opens the door for me; an invitation to step into my worst nightmare.

I gasped and made a guttural noise. My Luke was lying in the bed all pumped up and swollen, with a huge tube coming out of his mouth. Air hissed on and off, like a deadly snake. His lungs jerked up and down awkwardly. I touched his skin and although warm, it felt different. It felt as if he was no longer inside of it. I cried until I had nothing left inside to let go of.

'What have you done Luke? What have you done?' I asked him, even though I knew he could not answer.

I pulled a chair next to him and put my head next to his arm and I closed my eyes, willing him to wake up. I am emotionally exhausted as I close my eyes willing this nightmare away. An alarm screetches and before I can process what is happening I get eased out of the room as nurses and doctors rush in. I try to see through the blinds that had been tilted and I know this is not a good sign.

A nurse walked out of the room and ushered me into the family room. I registered another doctor coming into the room and words falling out of his mouth, words that my brain wanted to reject. Soon after the noise of a dying animal filled the room. I was so disorientated and wondered if I was dreaming. More words, soothing voices, a blanket draped across my shoulder; and just like that my life changed forever.

Luke was dead.

TWENTY-TWO

Dani

Sometime later mum rushed through the door.

'Darling girl, surely you can't go through anymore in your lifetime. I don't know what to say Dani other than I am so so sorry.'

I sat numb, frozen in grief as I tried to process what had just happened.

'Darling the police will want to speak to you. Have you talked to Craig yet?' I shook my head. 'I'll call him. I'll be back in a minute.' She disappeared; I have no idea how long for because time meant nothing to me anymore.

'Dani, Craig has suggested that you come clean and tell the police everything. Pez is dead now, so you no longer need to hide behind a false name. Craig will support you through it. All you have to do is call him.'

'Whatever,' I say. I can't even be bothered to think about whether I agree with that or not.

'Have you eaten Dani?' Mum asked.

'I'm not hungry.'

'I know but you have to eat darling.' She left the room and return with a pre-packaged egg sandwich and a small bottle of water.

Time drifted strangely with some minutes feeling like hours and some hours passing like seconds. Nothing made sense anymore. I looked around me as we drove from the airport to mum's house and suddenly everything looked different.

It was as if my world had actually tilted, and I was viewing things from a strange angle.

I walked into the house and Elanor hugged me as I came through the door. No words were exchanged between us, but we had a silent understanding. Chadd ran up to me, unaware that his world had changed forever.

'Mummy, Mummy! Where's daddy?' I looked into his innocent little eyes and broke down. I had no idea how to do this in a way that would not confuse or upset him. As if reading my mind Elanor said, 'Some conversations need to take place no matter how hard.'

I kneeled opposite him and wiped the tears that were free falling from my eyes. 'Chadd, I have to tell you something about daddy.' I closed my eyes for a second, gathering strength. 'Daddy can't come home darling because he got very sick in hospital, and he went to heaven baby.'

His little brow furrowed in confusion. 'But I want dad.' He said, in a voice that implied he was not going to settle for anything less than his father in person.

'So do I baby,' I said, and I felt as if someone had just hit me with a sledge hammer in the chest.

The police arrived at the house a few hours later and I accompanied them to the police station where I told them everything.

They were very supportive of what I had been through and offered me counselling through victims of crime. I declined but said I would think about it once the funeral was over. The officer I spoke to informed me that Pez (Peree Ezpinossa) and Marcus Tompson (Gunner) had both been shot. Pez was dead and Gunner was on life support. The bullet had damaged his spine and if he did manage to survive, he was not expected to walk again.

I returned home and left mum and Elanor to deal with Chadd and the funeral. I knew it was selfish and I knew that I was running away but I felt weariness like never before. It was as if all of my life events crashed down upon me and sucked the very life right out of me. I lay on the bed and for the first time in a long time, I did not care if I woke up once I fell asleep.

Twenty-Three

Eva

I couldn't even begin to imagine how Dani must feel. On paper she'd been traumatised since her father had died, not to forget the unmentionable things that happened to her in the hands of that despicable man, and now this. It seemed Luke had loved Dani and Chadd that much that he had set them free from the hell that they were trapped in, but at the cost of his own life. Her withdrawal into herself was worrying. Even Elanor being here wasn't helping.

'Elanor I'm worried sick about her! She barely eating, she's sleeping all day and she refuses point blank to discuss anything about the funeral, which is in three-days time. Peter is being as supportive as he can be, but I can see his patience wearing thin. He keeps reminding me that Chadd needs his mother; as if I don't know that!'

'I'll try talking to her again Eva but every time I knock on her door, she either refuses to answer or tells me to come back later. She will barely even look at Chadd and the poor love doesn't know what is happening, It's almost like he lost two parents.'

'Leave it to me. I'm doing it now. She might not like me for this, but her son needs her.'

I marched up the stairs, my bravery waning with each step. I felt as if I was balancing on a seesaw with Dani. On one hand I'm scared that I will tip her over the edge. On the other hand, I think she needs a reality check because her little boy is also grieving.

I knocked on the door and don't wait for an invite to enter. I see Dani turn away and attempt to pull the covers over her head.

'I know you're awake Dani and this is hard for me. I know you are suffering, but so is Chadd. You have a little boy downstairs asking for both of his parents. Only one of you can give him what he needs - he needs love and reassurance from you. Despite how you feel you need to get out of bed and face this. You're strong Dani and you have us to support you. Don't lock yourself away, we are here for you.'

I left the room before the tears fell.

Thirty minutes later I heard Dani in the shower and not long after that she walked down the stairs. She looked so young with no make-up on dressed in pyjamas, wet patches on each shoulder, plaits hanging either side of her face. She was pale and anxiety seemed to follow her footsteps like a shadow, never far behind. I watched her play with Chadd but it as obvious that she was just going through the motions. Her eyes were empty, and everything seemed to take effort.

Maybe you could take Chadd out for some fresh air?' I suggested, tentatively.

'Maybe tomorrow,' she replied, without looking at me.

I swallowed down the fear that welled inside of me as I tried to envisage her moving forward and standing on her own two feet without Luke by her side.

TWENTY-FOUR

Dani

I sit at the table looking at the breakfast that had been placed in front of me, aware that my mother was sipping coffee in the kitchen watching me to see if I would eat. Food repulsed me at the moment, another symptom of grief that's invisible to others. Well, everyone except my mother.

'We have a big day darling, and it really is important that you line your stomach.'

I forced myself to bite some toast and swill it back with a drink of orange juice. I could feel the two wrestling to stay in my stomach as soon as they hit it. Today was Luke's funeral. I couldn't believe it was real, it seemed like another nightmare that I wished I could wake from, only I couldn't.

Chadd was staying with Elanor, and we were having a quiet service at a nearby church followed by a cremation. Luke had no family attending. The police had confirmed that his mum was in a nursing home and not well enough to travel. Luke had no other siblings and due to the decline in his mum's mental state they were unable to determine if there were any other family members. We concluded that the fewer people the better.

I saw the hearse pull up and felt my stomach flip. I wore a simple black dress and jacket with thick black tights and heels. I stepped out into the cold air and walked towards the car that carried my soul mate. As I pulled the seat belt over me and looked out of the window at the passing scenery, I forced my mind into a corner, far away from the reality of this day, closing the door on the pain.

The church service passed in a blur of dreadful singing, and I was thankful for the vicar's loud voice echoing around the empty church.

As we walked out of the church, a woman dressed in a fitted black dress and laboutin shoes stood to the left of the path. It was hard not to notice her because everything about her demanded attention, from her model like figure to her expensive outfit. She was holding the hand of a child who looked to be around seven years old. I looked at her and she grinned, not in a way that oozed empathy, more in a way that implied she was ecstatically happy. The boy started tugging on her arm. 'Wait one moment darling,' She drawled in what sounded like a Russian accent.

The police informed us two weeks later that Pez's fat sidekick had died. I got an update about the girls that had been held in the house at Wilmslow and was overjoyed to know that they were now free. Traumatised, but free!

Weeks passed with each day feeling more painful the longer that Luke was gone. I longed to hear his voice and have him tell me it was going to be OK. Everything annoyed me. People laughing on the street, people sitting in cafes drinking coffee and chatting, daring to show their own happiness, it drove me crazy. I wanted to scream to the world so people see could feel my pain. I wanted everyone that came into contact with me to understand, but that wasn't possible, so I avoided going out and having happiness shoved down my throat.

Chadd was having tantrums on a regular basis. He was seeing a child therapist who assured me it was just his way of processing and coming to terms with the loss of his father. I all felt too familiar and it just reminded me of Australia, and Luke and I worrying ourselves sick about him. Only now it was just me, and that felt terrifying.

I felt sucked into a black cloud that weighed me down with exhaustion and negativity. No matter how much I tried to climb out of it, I couldn't seem to manage. Sometimes I felt as if the black cloud was an actual hand that was choking me.

It was three weeks later when that cloud slowly started to disperse.

'Dani, this may be a strange question, but I just wondered if there was any chance that you could be pregnant?' Mum asked.

My numb brain fired up and I realised that I'd not had a period since before Luke died but grief did that.

'I don't think so,' I said, hesitantly. 'What made you ask?'

'You've been off your food and feeling sick.'

'Maybe I should do a test to find out.'

Later that day I sat looking at two lines on a plastic stick and the word pregnant staring back at me. I wasn't sure how I felt, but for the first time since Luke had died a tiny bubble of hope formed within me. I was pregnant with Luke's baby.

The next four months were a flurry of doctors' appointments, scans, and baby buying, which definitely helped me fight my way out of the darkness. I was six months pregnant by that stage with a baby girl. I went through a rollercoaster of emotions feeling excited one moment, and devastated the next because Luke would not be able to be a part of her life. Chadd didn't fully understand what was happening but at almost four he was old enough to understand that I had a baby in my tummy, and he was going to be a big brother. It gave us all something positive to focus on.

Fourteen weeks later at twenty-one minutes past midnight, our beautiful baby girl entered the world. I named her Laila, which meant *of the night*.

TWENTY-FIVE

Dani

Fourteen Years Later

Laila bounced down the stairs face covered in make-up. Make-up so thick I could almost have written my name in it.

'You're not going out like that!' I said.

'Am.' She replied confidently with a hint of attitude thrown in. I was sure my daughter had been sent to try every ounce of patience I had. She'd gone from a sweet friendly girl to a demon teen overnight. Eye rolling replaced smiles and tuts and huffs were the newest sound addition.

'Laila, you are not going out with that amount of make-up on, it looks terrible. You're fifteen not eighteen, now go and take it off.'

She stomped up the stairs and I caught mutterings of how much she hated me before she slammed her bedroom door, sending a shudder through the house.

Ten minutes later she came back down, make-up mostly removed but now the skirt had been hitched up a notch. I sighed, unwilling to start another fight with her.

'Be in by eight please.' She flicked me a look that oozed teenage contempt and I remembered how I had been with my mum. It scared me now that I was the one in the firing line.

Chadd was in his room on a computer. I knocked and entered when he spoke.

'Do you know what's up with your sister? She's got attitude in the bucket load lately and I don't know why. And what time are you at college tomorrow?'

'No idea what's up with her. I start at ten.' Chadd, my laid-back boy was so different to Laila. She was fiercely stubborn, passionate, and always on the go. Chadd would go with the flow, and nothing seemed to faze him, whereas Laila needed an outline of what was happening and when. Up until the past two months she had mostly been a good kid. Yes, we clashed from time to time, but she had never been as challenging as this. I put it down to it being a teenage thing but now I wondered if there was more to it. Maybe she was being bullied, which spurred me to do something I swore I would never do. I went into her bedroom looking for evidence of 'something' to justify this change in her.

I looked in her chest of drawers, nothing, so I checked her bedside drawer and found a piece of paper. I unfolded it and looked at the red heart and the words encased inside of it: LAILA LOVES SEB. Well, that explained the change in attitude, shorter skirt and caked on make-up.

At eight pm there was no sign of Laila and she wasn't answering her phone. It was times like this that I missed Luke the most. I had no one to sound off to, no one to tell me it would be OK, and despite knowing that pushing boundaries was a normal part of growing up, my mind still ran away with itself.

When Laila was born, we had lived with mum for the first year of her life and then I bought a house in Harrogate. To this day I had no idea why I chose there, maybe because I could feel anonymous and that really appealed at the time. It worked though, and the children and I slowly made a life for ourselves. They knew nothing about what had happened in my past. It wasn't that I'd never wanted to tell them, it was just such an awkward topic to bring up, and it never seemed like the time was right. I mean, how do you break it to your children that you were involved in drugs, held hostage, raped, forced into prostitution, and that was the reason their dad was no longer with us. I couldn't bring myself to do it for fear of it changing our relationship. The thought of them looking at me differently would break me.

There had been no one else in my life since Luke, I just couldn't. He had been my healer, the man that knew my past and accepted me anyway. He had been able to soothe me when I was transported back there and he could bring me back to the present. I knew that no one else out there could do that, and I didn't even want to try looking for a substitute. I was happy just having my children around me.

Mum and Peter were living in Barcelona in a beautiful villa, and the children and I spent most of the school holidays there. I was working as a free-lance writer having secured a slot with a local newspaper. I had sent in a post about sexual assault and how there was little or no support out there for victims, and had been offered a small paragraph slot on a weekly basis, which over time had grown. I worked for myself and worked from home, so I was always here if the children needed me. It was perfect.

I did the whole 'school mom' thing whenever I had to and occasionally met up with a few of the mums for coffee, but I kept enough distance to never let anyone close enough to pry.

I checked my watch, and it was now eight thirty. I called Laila's phone and left a message telling her to consider herself grounded. She eventually walked through the door at nine fifteen as if nothing was wrong.

'Where the hell have you been?'

'Oh, God! Chill out mother!'

'Chill out mother!' I shouted. 'Chill out mother!'

'Wow, I heard you the first time, and so did all of the neighbours.' A smirk formed on her top lip and for the first time since she was four years old when she had ran out in front of a car, I felt like hitting her.

'Go to your room and you won't be going out for the next week at least, and if you don't drop the attitude you won't be going back out at all.' I said, quietly but firmly.

'I can't wait to leave home!' She yelled as she ran up the stairs in tears, followed by the obligatory door slam.

Chadd walked down the stairs a look of surprise on his face, right at the moment when Laila walked to the top of the stairs and started screaming that I had been in her room, and she couldn't believe how disgusting I was for going through her stuff and how this house was totally worse than being in prison. She ended it by saying how maybe if I got my own life I wouldn't be such a stalker and sad loser. I was wounded! I'd had a vision in my head of being the total opposite of my mother. I had pictured myself hanging out with my daughter, having dinner dates and laughing at the same movies. Instead, I was living in a war zone.

'Woah, what's with the kick offs in this house lately?' Chadd asked.

'All I know is your sister has a boyfriend and she's grounded because she was over an hour late and refused to answer her phone.'

'It can't be anyone from our school because I would have heard about it from my mates. Most of them have brothers or sisters still there.'

'If you do hear anything, let me know please. I'm worried about her.'

I wondered for the millionth time if being a parent ever got easier.

TWENTY-SIX

Laila

There he was again, waiting outside of the school gates staring at me. The first time he'd been there, looking at *me*, I'd thought he was looking at someone else. I looked around to see who else was there but there was just Tayla and I.

Tayla had nudged me 'He's staring at you,' she'd whispered, and giggled. I'd blushed and tried not to look at him, but I couldn't help it. He'd winked and I'd turned the colour of a tomato much to Tayla's amusement.

He always parked in the same place so that I was forced to walk past him and today I was on my own because Tayla was off school sick. My heart was racing the closer I got and even though I wasn't looking at him I could feel his eyes boring a hole in me.

'Hey sexy'.

Oh my god, no one had ever called me sexy. I felt a mixture of embarrassment and euphoria. He opened the car door and stepped out.

'Don't go.' He said, and my heart raced faster than it ever had. I hesitated, unsure what to do.

'What do you want?' I asked, nerves causing my voice to quiver.

'I like you.' He flashed a smile, and my stomach did a somersault as I looked at him. He was the sexiest thing I'd ever seen; ripped muscles, tattoos, and a smile to die for. He looked about twenty. My mum would freak if she knew he was even looking at me, let alone talking to me.

'I have to go,' I said, panicking and feeling even younger than my fifteen years next to him.

'Can I have your number?' He asked, and I faltered.

'Erm, I don't have my phone with me sorry.' I fidgeted with my school bag and stood there unsure what to do next.

'Another day.' He winked and cracked a smile that almost made me pass out.

'Bye.' I waved awkwardly as I walked off, cheeks flushed, heart racing like a steam train.

He started waiting outside of the school at least three days every week, and it was causing a bit of a stir. Older girls vied for his attention, but he remained fixated on me, which was both embarrassing and amazing.

On Monday at school the following week I thought about him all day. It was like my drug fix walking out of school and seeing his car, my heart would skip a beat and then he would wink at me or try to speak, but I always walked away from him. Today I had decided that I was finally going to give him my mobile number.

I gave myself a quick squirt of *Jo Malone - Orange Blossom*, which I'd taken from my mum's room and would be in serious trouble for if she found out. I walked out of the school gates and stopped short because his car wasn't there. It was always here on a Monday, every week without fail. I was devastated.

It was the same the following day, and the rest of the week; my mystery man had disappeared, and I had no way of getting in touch with him. I didn't even know his name, but I felt as if I loved him.

The weekend dragged miserably, each second lasting an hour until eventually Monday came around. I watched the time tick by until final bell at three pm and I raced out of the class, legs walking as fast as possible without breaking into a sprint, and I see him standing against his car, dressed in black jeans and a black t-shirt with a skull on the front. His arms were crossed as if impatient but as I get closer to him, I can see that he is smiling at me. Happiness bursts inside of me like tiny bubbles. This time when he looked at me and used his finger to gesture for me to go to him, I did.

'Did you miss me?'

I blushed, dumbstruck by him, and in awe of the invisible cord that pulled me toward him.

'So can I have your mobile number now?' He asked, and this time I didn't hesitate to give him it. There was no way I ever wanted to feel that sense of hopelessness again. He looked so pleased with himself as he got back in his car and drove off without saying anything, leaving me feeling confused. He'd not said anything other than asking for my number. Usually, he tried to coax me into going for a drive or he asked how my day had been. I felt deflated after waiting all weekend. I needn't have worried though because an hour later my mood rocketed as a text came through from him. *See you soon gorgeous* it said. The relief I felt was overwhelming.

That night as I lay in bed, I couldn't stop thinking about him. The mystery man whose name I didn't even know. My phone chimed, as if he was able to tap into my thoughts. I read the message. *I can't stop thinking about you. I think you are the most beautiful girl I have ever seen. Seb x*

His name was Seb, short for Sebastian, he was twenty-two years old, and he thought I was beautiful. He literally turned my life upside down with that text. I started making a huge effort when I went to school. I got up extra early and washed and dried my hair and put make up on, in the hope that he would be waiting at the end of the day. All I could think about at school was *him*, and in place of literature and algebra, Seb filled my thoughts. He would call me at night or message me on Facebook. My mum would flip if she knew I was using Facebook when I was supposed to be sleeping, but it was like I was addicted to him and the attention that he showered upon me. He would talk to me about us being together one day, and how he would take me travelling. He said we would sleep under the stars, free spirits that would be governed by the moon and the sun. I had never met anyone like him.

Sometimes he would send me a picture of him lying in bed with just his boxer shorts on, I would blush bright red, thankful that he was not in the same room as me, and he would ask me to send him a picture. I always said no because I was too embarrassed, but it didn't stop him asking. He had started turning up some mornings at school and had asked me twice if I would skip school and go for a ride with him. I never agreed because I knew I would be grounded forever if mum found out, but I was aware that I sounded like a child. He would get this look on his face as if he was annoyed with me, and some days he would just drive off without speaking. I would feel sick on those days.

I had agreed to meet Seb one night at the shopping centre car park. I told mum I was going out with friends, but she was starting to be such a control freak, telling me to take my make-up off before I went out. That night she started ringing me at five past eight; it was so embarrassing. There was no way I was telling Seb I had to be home by eight, so I switched my phone off. She went ape shit when I got in, shouting at me telling me I was grounded and then I saw my piece of paper on the bedside cabinet, the one I'd drawn love hearts on.

'I can't believe you have been in my bedroom going through my drawers like a total stalker! Oh my god, what is wrong with you? You seriously need to get a life mum and maybe then you'll stop obsessing over mine!'

Now I was grounded. How the hell was I meant to explain that to Seb without looking ridiculous? I couldn't wait until I was old enough to do what I wanted!

The following morning mum was waiting in the kitchen as usual, lunch boxes all prepped in the fridge, benches wiped down and crumb free as she pushed a bowl of cereal towards me. I couldn't bring myself to look at her and I was still pissed that she had been snooping in my room.

Chadd threw himself on to one of the breakfast stools and started shovelling food into his mouth. God boys of his age were so gross, all they did was eat, sleep, and game. How boring!

'Make sure you don't leave anything in your room that you don't want mum to see Chadd, because she'll be in there sniffing around when you leave for school.'

'That's enough Laila. If you hadn't switched your phone off I wouldn't have needed to go in your room.' Mum said, lips pursed as if holding herself back from losing it again.

'Yeah right.' I snorted, as I jumped off the stool and grabbed my lunch from the fridge.

'Laila. Listen, for what it's worth I am sorry about going into your room, I know it's not a cool thing to do, but I was worried about you. You don't understand what it's like being a parent, and when you didn't answer your phone, I panicked.'

'Seriously mum, I know with dad it must have been hard for you and everything, but you should go to talk to someone about that because you can't stop us from growing up and living a life.' I walked out hoping that she would back the hell off and allow me to just be a teenager.

When I returned home later that day, she was waiting for me.

'So, would you like to tell me about your boyfriend? I don't want to fall out with you baby, I want you to be able to come to me and tell me things.'

'Mum, you do know that no one does that right? None of my friends confide in their parents, and when they do it's fake anyway. Do you think we're going to sit down with you and tell you about all of the things we know you'll disagree with?' Mum looked shocked and hurt, before muttering about *this parent thing being way harder than she'd ever imagined.*

'Well, OK then, I would like it if you could talk to me about *some* things.'

She would not let this go. I looked at her and felt a bit sorry for her. She had absolutely no life my mum, just an unhealthy obsession with what Chadd and I were up to. She never went anywhere and even worked from home. She lived in this one-way perspex box where she could look out onto the world, but no one could look in. It simply wasn't healthy to keep living like that and put all her energy and focus on to us. She kept pretending she'd been this cool teenager herself but all I saw was a stress head who wasn't prepared to let me grow up.

'He's not my boyfriend just so you know. We only talk.'

She looked relieved but I didn't hang around for the second round of questioning, I made a quick exit to my room.

Seb and I continued to text and talk over the next few months, I had been out with him in his car and we had kissed a few times, but I could sense he was getting impatient. It was approaching my sixteenth birthday and he was pressuring me to meet my mum. I'd told him about my dad dying and to be honest it was weird talking about this person who was such a big part of my life, yet someone I'd never even met.' Seb had not said a lot other than he knew how that felt. When I questioned him, he changed the subject. On the day of my birthday my mum surprised me with a Pandora necklace. We were going out for a meal to a local Italian restaurant later that day and gran and Peter were joining us. They had flown back just for my birthday.

'I'd like Sebastian to come tonight if that's OK?' She spun around on the spot and stared at me before grabbing her bag.

'Tell Sebastian to be at the restaurant for seven pm, I have to go and pick a few things up in town. Your bus will be here in ten minutes, have a lovely day at school birthday girl and I'll see you later.'

Fast forward a few hours and I felt sick with nerves. We were all waiting on Seb and he was late. Mum hated people who were late and I could see her checking her watch. I was now thinking that this was the most ridiculous idea ever. Why had I not suggested he come to the house at the weekend? I didn't have long to stress though because he walked in, confident and so bloody handsome that I couldn't stop looking at him. Peter coughed, bringing me back to the here and now, and I blushed bright red. I stood up nervously, unsure of my new role as girlfriend in front of my family. I felt awkward.

'Mum, everyone, this is Sebastian.' I was thankful that he had worn a long-sleeved grey shirt to hide his tattoos.

Gran seemed reserved. 'Nice to meet you.' She said, but I sensed it was anything *but* nice.

Mum glared at him openly. 'Hello Sebastian,' she said rather curtly. I looked at her squinting my eyes in annoyance.

He had no sooner sat down when mum started quizzing him, How old are you? Do you have a job? Where do you work? How long have you known my daughter? Where do you live? How did you meet? Oh my god she just kept going. It was so uncomfortable.

'Can you stop." I snapped, then softened my voice. 'Please. It's my birthday I just want to have a nice time.'

'Sorry,' she said, but I could tell that she wasn't.

We left the restaurant and as soon as we got home mum found her voice again.

'We need to talk about Sebastian, Laila.'

I rolled my eyes.

'You can leave the attitude at the door young lady.' Silence. I looked away even though I knew that she was staring at me. 'He's too old for you.' We had agreed to say that he was eighteen, but it was clear she didn't buy it.

'I knew you didn't like him!' I said, angrily before storming upstairs. 'Thanks for a lovely birthday,' I yelled down the stairs. I picked my phone up and I had two missed calls from Seb. I dialled his number.

'Your mum hates me, doesn't she?' He said as soon as he answered.

'No honestly, she's like that with everyone.' The words just came out of my mouth without thinking, but I wondered if she was and maybe I hadn't noticed.

'Are you sure? Maybe it would be better if we just ended this, especially if your mum is against us.' Seb said, causing panic to swell within me. I spent the next thirty minutes trying to reassure Seb that mum wasn't a monster and that she did like him.

'OK, well can I come to your house on the weekend?'

Oh crap this was getting awkward.

'I'll speak to mum,' I muttered, already dreading the conversation. '

'Well, if she likes me as you say, there'll be no issue.' He concluded.

Fuck. How would I get out of this now?

The following morning I felt stressed. Mum was trying to be nice and while part of me wanted to be nice back, I was also annoyed that she had created an issue when there really shouldn't be one.

'Sebastian would like to come over on the weekend.'

She closed her eyes as if willing my words away. 'I'll have a think about it. I'm not sure Chadd is keen on him so I'll have to see.'

'You mean you're the one not keen!'

'Please Laila. I don't want to keep arguing with you. You have your whole life ahead of you, you're too young for a boyfriend at this age, especially someone older than you!'

'How old were you when you first got a boyfriend mum?'

'Don't change the subject, we're talking about you and don't think that your gran didn't have this conversation with me. Eighteen my eye! He's more like twenty-two plus.'

'Yeah, well this is my house too and he's coming over.' I said before leaving for school. I just couldn't be bothered with her parent chatter battering my brain. I could hear her freaking out as I left the house but that was short lived because as I walked down the drive toward the bus stop Seb was waiting on me. My stomach did that flip thing as soon as I saw him and he opened the door of the passenger seat and I climbed in. Two girls from the year above me stood who stood with their mouths open. I felt so grown up and cool. Seb leant over, looked at them, kissed me on the lips and then squeezed my left breast rendering me speechless.

'That will give them something to think about, jealous little girls clearly wishing they were as sexy as you.'

I was in turmoil, burning with a mixture of embarrassment and arousal. How the hell was I supposed to concentrate at school now? He pulled up the car a few lanes back from my school and kissed me passionately, probing his tongue in my mouth, alerting every nerve ending in my body that I was well and truly alive. He grazed my nipple through my shirt again and I groaned.

'Do you have any idea how much I want you? How much I think about you, you're almost driving me crazy Lai.' I loved that he called me that, nobody called me that but him. I was still catching my breath when he looked at me in the eye.

'Skip school spend the whole day with me. I'll take you somewhere special.' He nuzzled my neck sending shivers through me.

'I'll get in trouble,' I said, instantly regretting how lame it sounded.

'Aww will you get sent to bed early?' He mocked, making me feel about five years old. He could tell I was upset, and he kissed me again until I couldn't think straight.

'Please, I'm not asking again. We're supposed to be a couple and we've talked for months but other than take me to the family dinner, which was not a nice experience, it's like you don't want to be around me.'

'I do want to be around you, of course I do, it's just school,' my voice trailed off because again I was making myself sound childlike.

'So, if you want to, why not do it? Like I say I'm not going to ask again, there's only so many times a guy can ask before feeling as if he's getting the brush off.' He made it sound like an ultimatum. I thought back to when he disappeared for a week, and I couldn't stand the thought of not seeing him.

'OK.' I said before I could even process what I was doing. Seb let out a whoop and put his seat belt back on.

'Buckle up baby, I'm about to take you on the ride of your life.'

He was so happy I couldn't help but feel it too. I would face the consequences later; say I was upset about the argument I had with mum so I spent the day at the park trying to figure it all out.

My stomach was filled with butterflies as we drove to wherever we were going. Seb was grinning from ear to ear and repeatedly telling me how happy he was that I'd finally agreed to go with him. I was buzzing with nervous energy and something else that I'd never experienced before, and it felt amazing.

Seb pulled up at a shop and came out with a bag of food and some alcohol. I wasn't sure what was happening, and I felt stupid asking, so I sat quietly accepting that he was older and knew best, and I trusted him.

We drove for miles and eventually ended up on a dirt track that seemed to go on forever. We pulled up outside at an old property that looked unused. The house had paint flaking from the wooden windows frames with glass that gave no reflection, due to the build-up of grime.

'Who lives here?' I asked, feeling grossed out.

'It belongs to my friend. He moved out of the area for a while; let's just say that he's otherwise occupied in a different kind of house.'

I had no idea what he meant but I wasn't feeling keen to step inside. Seb looked at me and laughed.

'Don't worry babe, we're going up there,' he pointed to a hill. 'It's the best view for miles and absolutely no one around, so we can do whatever we want,' he added with a wink. My stomach did a somersaulted in anticipation and adrenalin flooded my body as uncertainty replaced excitement.

Seb grabbed the food and drink and a blanket from the car, and we marched our way up the hill, each step causing my breath to falter with nerves. I was starting to feel a little out of my depth and I now wished that I'd just gone to school.

Seb lay the blanket down and opened a bottle of wine, producing two plastic beakers. He filled them both to the brim and handed me one. I took it not wanting to look stupid, but I had never drunk before.

'You know Lai, the thing I love about you,' My mind went crazy because he had just said *love*. I played the sentence back in my head *the thing I love about you*. He snapped a finger in front of me 'Hey where'd you go to?' He laughed.

'Sorry,' I said flushing again. I wished my face would stop doing that.

'I was saying, the thing I love about you is that you're not like the other girls, you're cool. Like today, you did what you wanted to do, not what your mum *makes* you do. You have a mind of your own and that is what I find so sexy.' He gently pushed me down and kissed me, while he unbuttoned my shirt. He slipped his hand inside my bra, grazing my nipple in the flesh causing me to gasp. Before I could gain awareness of what was happening, he unhooked my bra and peeled his lips from my mouth and placed them around my nipple. My god my whole body was screaming out for him, but he pulled away and sat up, handing me more wine. 'Drink, you'll like it, it's what all the cool girls drink. It's Moscato.' Numb from what had just happened I tilted the cup and allowed the cold liquid to slip down my throat as he watched me. I went to fasten my top.

'Don't, I want to look at you, I could look at you all day and night.' I felt as if things were moving too fast but I felt unable to stop this happening.

I watched him lay food out, nothing flash, a few sausage rolls from the deli counter, and a bag of crisps and some peanuts.

'You like your wine?' He asked, bottle ready to top up. 'Empty your cup first.' He said, so I knocked back the remainder in the cup while watching him fill it back up.

We ate a little and he kept pouring me more and more wine, telling me how amazing I was, and how he loved me, and how mature I was compared to other girls my age.

'Like, some girls your age wouldn't even let a boy touch their breasts, that's how immature they are.' I sat silent feeling torn between the two sides of me. One voice telling me to leave now, the other part of me revelling in the compliments that Seb was showering me with.

I was starting to feel woozy and silly. I hugged him hanging off his neck giggling before kissing him.

'Take off your shirt Lai.'

I was like a deer caught in the headlights, unsure which direction to take. While I was trying to decide, Seb peeled my shirt off leaving me totally naked from the waist upwards. He muttered to himself about my amazing breasts before bending to kiss them. I felt such a mixture of emotions it was making me dizzy. He unzipped my skirt pulling it down around my ankles and I fell lazily onto the blanket in a drunken stupor. I was trapped now, too scared to make him stop and so eager to make him happy, but I knew that we were about to have sex and I hadn't really planned on that. He took out his mobile phone and took a picture of me lying almost naked. I tried to ask him why and it was almost like he'd read my mind.

'I need to see you anytime I want to baby. I hate being away from you, this way I get to stare at your beauty any time of day or night and you have no idea how happy that makes me feel. We had sex, it was over quickly and afterwards I wondered if I had dreamt it because I woke up and my clothes were on.

'Hello sleeping beauty.' I opened my eyes to Seb looking at me with a grin on his face.

'What times is it?' I asked, feeling nausea claw at my throat. I looked at the two empty bottles of wine and started to retch. I was certain that Seb had drank most of it. I didn't feel too good though, and I still had to go home and face mum and Chadd. I prayed that school had not rung my mum to query my absence.

'It's quarter to two. Do you think we should head back?'

'Yes, but how can you drive? You've been drinking.'

He laughed and ruffled my hair. 'Spoken like a true child.'

Ouch! That hurt me and he must have seen it written on my face, he pulled me to him.

'Sorry, you know you're not a child don't you, you're definitely all woman, you just proved it,' he winked, and I turned puce. 'Don't be embarrassed baby, you were amazing and next time will be even better and hopefully there will be no tears.'

Holy shit, I'd cried? I couldn't remember a thing. How cringe.

'We'll stop at maccas on the way home and you can get a burger and some coffee and then I'll drop you near your house.'

I stepped out of the car near home and my heart was hammering but I needn't have worried because mum clearly knew nothing about my day off school. I had used the automated system as Seb had suggested and it seemed to have worked. *Press 1 for absences and leave the student's name, year, and class.* I felt a bit of a buzz at the fact I had got away with it and when I told Seb he suggested we do it again.

The next day at school was a nightmare. Tayla was back at school, and she walked past me in the yard with another girl called Jasmine, and she barely glanced at me. I got a strange sinking feeling in my stomach and ran after them trying to convince myself that maybe she hadn't seen me, even though I was certain she had.

'Hi.'

Tayla spun around quickly; anger written on her face.

'Is it true? Did you have sex in that man's car in front of people yesterday?'

My mouth fell open and colour drained from my face. 'No what are you talking about?' A memory of Seb squeezing my breast and the words *that will give them something to talk about* popped into my head making me turn the colour of a ripe tomato.

'If you've done nothing wrong, why are you bright red?' She probed angrily. A group of girls walked past us and joined in.

'Eww keep away from the slapper, she has sex in cars with men.' I heard them giggle as they walked away.

For the rest of the day I had to endure comments and jibes about how much I charged by the hour along with some unpleasant name-calling. I had never felt so alone in my life. I spent lunch hour by myself in a corner of the field as far away from others as I could get.

TWENTY-SEVEN

Dani

I'd not had a chance to catch up with mum since the meal, but I knew that she had been as shocked as I had when Laila's boyfriend had walked into the restaurant. I was old enough to know that he was bad news and he was older than eighteen, despite Laila's insistance.

I looked at the words swimming on the computer screen in front of me and closed the lid of my laptop. It was no good, I just couldn't concentrate. I needed to speak to mum, and I wasn't sure if I needed reassurance or clarification that my instincts were right.

'Mum, sorry I meant to call you the day after Laila's birthday, but I've been busy, and I've also been stewing this whole thing over. What do you think of this boyfriend that Laila's hanging around with? She wamts Sebastian to come over at the weekend and I don't know about you, but I think he's bad for her. There's been a change in her attitude since she met him.'

'I did think he seemed a bit old but if you push her to hard Dani, you will push her right into his arms. I can't tell you what to do darling, you're her mum and you do whatever you think is right.'

'That's the thing mum, I have no idea what right is. I hate being alone and having to make all of these decisions. I wish Luke was here.' My heart ached for a few seconds as I let the pain out, before shutting the door on it again.

'Maybe get to know him a bit better first, and then decide whether he is good for her or not. At least that way you don't risk alienating her.'

'You're right. I need to take a step back and stop assuming he is guilty of being a bad influence when I don't really know him. Trusting men is something I will never get a handle on, hence why I am single.'

'Understandable darling after everything you've been through.' Mum soothed.

I end the call after a quick catch up and go back into my office to finish my writing column, which was due in today. I was in the middle of typing up my rough draft when my mobile rang for the second time.

There was a voice message from Laila's school from her year tutor, asking me to call her back as soon as possible. My heart rate escalated as I dialled the number.

'Hi, it's Laila Johnston's mum here, I had a missed call from Mrs Gregg.' I said to the admin lady. I was placed on hold and waited with bated breath for the teacher to pick up.

'Mrs Johnstone thank you for returning my call. I was ringing to check how Laila was doing today.'

'I'm sorry I don't understand, Laila is at school today.'

'Mrs Johnston would you be able to come into the school for a chat? Laila is not in school today, and she has missed quite a few days over the recent weeks which is out of character for her, hence the phone call to you.'

I knew automatically that she must be with that boyfriend of hers.

When I arrived at the school I was confronted with an impressive list of telephone absences, supposedly from myself to the school, as well two letters requesting that Laila be allowed to leave school early to attend medical appointments. There had been an obvious decline in her behaviour, and it appeared that she was no longer friends with the group of girls she usually hung around with. Credit to Mrs Gregg who had already spoken to Laila's friends to try and find out what was happening.

I got back into my car and dialled Laila's number – no answer. I waited outside of the school until her best friend Tayla came out.

'Tayla,' I shouted, catching her attention. She walked towards me slowly. 'Can I give you a lift home please, I need to talk to you about Laila.' She hesitated, but after saying bye to the girls she was walking with, she let herself into the passenger seat. I pulled the car away from prying eyes, already feeling my face burn with embarrassment that I no longer knew my daughter and was having to probe her friends for information about what was going on.

I pulled into a street that led into an overgrown grassy area and parked at the end of the road where it was quiet.

'Tayla what's going on? I find out today that Laila has been skipping school and that she has also fallen out with you. Why? What's happened?'

She squirmed in her seat, clearly uncomfortable. I dropped the window to get some air and steady my racing heart.

'She's got this boyfriend and, well, she's changed since she met him.' Tayla said, awkwardly.

'I know about Sebastian but why did you two fall out? You've been friends since you were five. What did you fall out about, please tell me.' She blushed and looked at the floor.

'There are rumours. Some others from our group saw her and Seb kind of having sex in the car.'

Oh my fucking god. I was speechless and devastated in equal measures. 'Where was this and when?' I asked, in a whisper.

'It was near the bus stop and he was kissing her, touching her here,' she pointed to her breasts and I could see how uncomfortable she was. 'He said it would give people something to talk about.'

'I'm so sorry for asking you these questions Tayla but I'm trying to figure it all out. Did you and her argue about that?'

'Yeah, people were calling her names at school but even before that, he was always hanging around and trying to get her to talk to him and asking her to get in his car. Then once she got with him, she just talked about him *all* the time.'

I wondered how much of this fall out was jealousy and how much was genuine hurt that Jasmine had abandoned her.

'Do you have any idea where she might be?' I asked.

She shook her head. 'I don't, sorry.'

I dropped Tayla off at home and give her a hug. 'Thankyou. I really appreciate your honesty.'

I drove off in shock, trying to process the fact that my daughter was the talk of the school for all of the wrong reasons.

I made myself a camomile tea and tried to settle my nerves as I waited on Laila coming home, unable to think or focus on anything else other than her walking through the door. Chadd rushed in at the usual time and walked straight to the fridge for food.

'Is something wrong?' His perfectly smooth skin creased at the brow as he waited for me to respond.

'No honey, I'm fine.' I lied. 'Have you seen your sister?'

'Nope. She wasn't on my bus.' he said. I zone out as he tells me about his day at college, and all I can do is watch the drive and wonder how I will manage to have a conversation with her without Chadd overhearing.

Twenty minutes later I watch Laila saunter up the driveway with a smile on her face and I feel my stomach sink. She's in love; it's written all over her dreamy expression.

She slammed the door behind her, hung her school bag on the rack and walked through to the kitchen.

'Hi,' She breezed, brightly. She was texting on her phone and I was tempted to take it off her and stamp on it.

'How was school?' I asked, watching her for a flicker of concern.

'Fine,' she smiled as she looked me in the eye, and I felt sick that she could lie so easily.

'Sit down.' I ordered, annoyance taking over at her lack of care. She looked at me and twisted her mouth into a snarl, ready to arc up.

'What's up with YOU?' She questioned cheekily, emphasizing the word you as she slumped in a chair.

'What's up with me madam, is that I had to go to your school and speak to your teacher today.' Her face paled slightly. 'I know you have been with Sebastian when you should have been at school, so what I want to know is, where have you been, and more to the point what the hell have you been doing?' Part of me hoped I would never found out the latter.

She stood up quickly to avoid having the discussion.

'Don't walk away from me Laila. I asked you where you have been today?'

'Why do you blame everything on Seb and anyway how do you even know I have been with him?' She responded defensively.

'Well seeing as you are not speaking to any of your friends, I figured you haven't been skipping school to go hang out with the homeless!'

She tutted and opened her mouth to speak but nothing came out.

'Incidentally, why *aren't* you speaking to your friends?'

'It's like Seb says, they're all jealous!'

'Jealous!' I shouted. 'Jealous of what Laila? Jealous of you almost having sex in a car with a man far too old for you? Or jealous that you are skipping school and falling behind on your grades?'

She turned the colour of beetroot and ran upstairs. I followed behind her conscious that I had lost all control of the situation and my emotions.

'You've always hated Seb, he knows, you know.' She said turning to face me, her face contorted with anger, momentarily scaring me for a second. My whole world suddenly felt too small. In the space of a few hours I felt as if I no longer knew my own child. My family, the one security blanket I wore with pride, had suddenly been ripped from beneath me and I felt afraid.

I walked down the stairs, tears free-falling, my brain a mess of inner questions and confusion. I think ahead to tomorrow when I am supposed to send her off to school knowing that I can't trust her, knowing that she will probably walk around the school yard alone, and despite being upset with her, I can't help feel sorry for her. I want to shake her and hug her, all at the same time.

The following morning after I have shouted up to Laila for the tenth time, I climb the stairs and open the door, and she's not there.

'She left for school already.' Chadd shouted from his room.

'Was she dressed in her uniform?' I asked.

'Uhu.' He replied, looking at me like I had lost the plot.

'We had a fall out. Sorry If I seem a bit tense. I'll drive you to college if you're ready.'

'OK.' He said.

I drop Chadd off and on the way back I park my car near the school gates, so that I can wait on Laila arriving.

I watched the children file into school, some walking alone, looking weighed down by their school bags and life, some laughing and clearly loving life.

I see a black car pull up, a racer boy kind of car with tinted windows. I stepped out of my car, mixing in with a group of children who were jostling for pavement space. I walked up to the window and glanced inside. They were in there kissing each other's faces off. I felt my stomach flip as nausea rose in me like a tidal wave. The noise of traffic and children was drowned out by my heart that was pumping wildly in my ears. I knocked on the window and Laila spun around with a half-smile. She stopped, stunned to see me and then turned to Seb and mouthed something before she opened the car door firmly, pushing me out of the way. I looked at the fire in her eyes that spewed out hatred.

'Oh my god! What kind of weirdo are you?' She spat at me in a mixture of embarrassment and anger.

'I beg your par...'

'Do you even have any idea how embarrassing you are?' She shouted as she interrupted me.

I had never felt so mortified in my whole life. I looked around and sure enough there was a bit of an audience now, people silently elbowing each other to come and join in the show. I stayed silent despite the fact I was seething inside, and I looked at Seb, who was sat there like the cat that got the cream. If I didn't know any better, I would have said that he was loving every minute of this, which made no sense to me whatsoever because surely, he would want his girlfriend's mum on side.

The crowd dispersed quickly as the school bell chimed for first call. Laila said goodbye to Seb, flicked her hair and waltzed off.

Seb sat in his car watching all of this unfold. He wound down the window and smiled at me.

'I don't know what you think you're doing but I want you to stay away from my daughter. You're too old for her and a bad influence. She's changed drastically since she met you. And not in a good way!' Again, I am met with a smirk of satisfaction.

'She almost a woman and can make up her own mind I think. Now close the door otherwise I will have you for harassment.' He closed the window, revved his car and drove off.

Nausea clawed at my throat as I walked back to the car feeling lost and out of depth. I was losing my daughter and that terrified me because I had already lost enough.

Twenty-Eight

Laila

My luck had just run out. I'd walked in from school, well, not school, because I had been with Seb all day, but I walked into the house and my mother was waiting, and I thought everything was cool until she started yelling at me. She knew about Seb and I in the car and I have never been so embarrassed in my whole life. And now I was grounded. As for school, it was a nightmare with everyone whispering about me, and the only person that seemed to want to hang out with me was Alice, the girl with no friends.

The following day at school Tayla walked past me with Grace, and I marched up to her.

'What do you think you're doing telling my mother things about me? I thought we were supposed to be friends Tayla. I would never have betrayed you like that.'

'We *were* friends. I don't know who you are anymore Laila. You've changed so much since meeting that MAN you hang out with. Everyone is talking about you, and not in a good way, and you don't seem to care.'

'Stuff you.' I said, more to myself than to her. A feeling of loneliness encased me. I missed my friends, but I loved Seb, and it was apparent that the two did not mix. I looked at Alice, so desperate to be liked by someone, and I felt so sorry for her now that I knew how it felt to be ostracized.

'Come on Alice, let's go and get some lunch.' I said as I linked arms with her.

This friendship could really work in my favour. I would have a friend to hang out with at school and because Alice was a dream pupil Mum might relax a little, and then I could see more of Seb if she thought I was with Alice.

I introduced Alice to Mum at the end of the day and then I waved goodbye to her before arranging to meet her the following morning.

Seb was parked over the road with the window down. He watched my conversation with Mum and Alice and then whistled as we walked towards mum's car. I glanced at mum.

'Don't even think about it,' she said. I shook my head at Seb and then did the hand sign that meant phone me behind Mum's back. He winked and drove off.

I was expecting a huge lecture in the car but Mum remained silent and in some ways that was worse than having a blazing row with her. It felt awkward; *I* felt awkward and I wasn't sure what to say to her. Gran was waiting in the house and my stomach sank because I suspected it meant a double-pronged attack, and I wasn't wrong.

'We want you to stop seeing Sebastian,' Mum said. 'He's too old for you and clearly a bad influence. Since you have met him, you have managed to fall out with all of your friends, you've been skipping school, and your attitude is terrible. You can hand over your phone because it's clear I can't trust you, and when I think you've earnt my trust back, you will get the phone back, but I will be the judge of when that is.'

I was speechless, no phone *and* grounded. 'How long am I grounded for?'

'At least a month.' Mum said, looking pleased with herself.

'Fine, I'll stop seeing him, but if I do that am I allowed out?'

'No. You're grounded for skipping school and leaving the house this morning to go and see your boyfriend.'

'Whatever. Can I go now?' I asked nonchalantly. I could see their shocked faces trying to figure why I had been so agreeable. I still had an IPad and mum didn't know that I had Facebook, so I might not be able to see Seb yet, but I could certainly message him.

I went into my bedroom and started typing on my IPad.

You won't believe what my mum has done...

I was *ungrounded* now, and as far as mum was concerned, I had ended my relationship with Seb. She loved Alice and was very encouraging of us spending time together. Occasionally I felt bad that I was lying to mum but she just had no give in her when it came to Seb, so I had no option.

I picked my mobile out of my bag and waited for Seb to pick up.

'I'm on my way.' I said, smiling to myself.

'Did you ask Alice over to your house tomorrow?'

'Of course.' I said smugly.

'And when she leaves, you'll be asking if you can have a sleep over at hers?'

'Yep.'

'So, Saturday night you'll be all mine then?'

'I sure will.'

I met Seb at the park once a week, and then I walked back to the library ten minutes before my mum was due to pick me up. It was the only way to see him, apart from using Alice. Alice was the best decoy ever, and she didn't even know it. Because she spent so much time at my house, mum never questioned if I slept over at hers. It had started as a way to see Seb, I would invite her to mine, then pretend I was going to her house for tea, but I'd meet Seb instead. It worked brilliantly. Mum thought I'd found a lovely friend, and she thought I was studying once a week at the library. A few months ago, I started asking if Alice could sleep over at our house on a Friday, then every second week I asked if I could sleep at hers. The first few times I did stay so that if mum rang, my story would match up, but I'd managed to sneak four nights with Seb during that time.

It was weird because I'd grown really fond of Alice, but I knew that she wouldn't approve of Seb, so I kept him my little secret.

I sat on the cold park bench and pulled my jacket around me as the biting wind cut through the fabric, piercing my skin with invisible needles. The trees whispered to each other as the March wind whipped through them, carrying the bitterness of a long winter with it as if reluctant to let it go.

Seb ran across the grass, hidden beneath his hoody. He sat down next to me and pulled me towards his lips, kissing me passionately before passing me a small hipflask. He smelled like whiskey and musky aftershave. It was a heady mix.

'Here you go. A little something to warm you through.' He said, handing me the flask. I took a swig and balked at the hot burning liquid that was making its way to my stomach, warming me from the inside out.

'Urgh, I'm not sure I like that.' I grimaced.

He laughed and then we start talking about what we would do on Saturday night. Seb liked to call them our 'adventures'. I had never been to his house because he always arranged something else for us to do. On one occasion he had borrowed a friends camper van and we had toasted marshmallows and drank beer underneath the stars. Another time we camped out in a tent on the moors, which had been terrifying, but Seb had said that was all part of the fun. Twice we had slept in his car, which I hadn't been so keen on. I had asked if we could just go to his house, but he said that he loved being in a small space with me because he got to hold me closer. He was so romantic at times.

This weekend we were going on a drive somewhere special, only he wouldn't tell me where we were going.

'Laila, Alice is here.' Mum shouted up the stairs.

'Just tell her to come up.' I yelled back.

Alice ran up the stairs and bounded into my room which was unlike her. She was usually pretty reserved. Her blonde wavy hair was in bunches which made her look years younger than she was. 'Look what I have.' She grinned as she pulled out a new iPhone.

'Whoa that's so cool. I wish my mum would buy me one of those.'

Alice was an only child and got everything without even asking for it. Her parents were the nicest people and they had asked me if I wanted to go on holiday with them in August to France. Apparently one of the aunts owned a chateau and they spent three weeks there each summer. As lovely as it was of them to offer, the thought of being so far from Seb for three weeks made me feel anxious, but I would have to give them an answer soon.

We hung out for a few hours, taking pictures with different filters and listening to music while we attempted to contour our faces like Kylie Jenner. When Alice came to leave, I made a point of standing at the door and shouting 'See you later', before asking mum if I could sleep at her house.

'Yeah of course,' She replied, without lifting her head from her magazine. I packed my bag and when mum was on the phone, I managed to sneak some food into my backpack just in case we ended up in the middle of nowhere starving, which had happened once before.

At four pm I walked into the room and mum was glued to her usual spot at the dining table. 'I'm going mum.' I walked over to give her a hug.

'I'll give you a lift honey.' She stood and smoothed down the knitted dress that she was wearing.

'No it's OK, I'd rather walk I've eaten too much pasta this week.' She looked at me and raised her eyebrows.

'You're not dieting, are you?'

'No, don't be silly. I'm just looking after myself. See you tomorrow but it might be in the afternoon because we always stay up watching movies then have a lie in.'

'Have a lovely time, Laila.'

I breathed a sigh of relief as I walked down the drive, thankful that I'd managed to wriggle out of getting a lift. That would have been rather awkward being dropped off at Alice's house without an invite.

It takes me thirty minutes to walk to the library where Seb is waiting for me.

'Are we sleeping in your car tonight?'

'No so you can relax.' He smiled.

'Give me a clue where we are going, just a little one,' I begged.

He smiled and shook his head as we leave Harrogate. I zone out as I watch the landscape flash past the window. It starts to cut in dark as we drive through Carlisle. I could see the hills in the distance and it felt as if we were entering another world.

'Where are we going Seb? We've been driving forever.'

'Almost there babe, another twenty minutes or so and we'll be able to set up for the night.'

Set up for the night. What did that even mean? I hoped we weren't camping again because it was too cold for that.

He stopped at a petrol station and then got back into the car with a can of beer. I felt nerves growing in my stomach as I watch him driving and drinking at the same time. I'm scared to say anything because he'll say I'm being childish. Instead I asked for a drink and I necked the can so he can't drink anymore. He laughed a real belly laugh and tells me that he's proud of me.

We pull onto some grass and weave along a dirt track and Seb stops at a small office that looks to be nothing more than a shipping container. A few minutes later we pull up at a small unit not much bigger than my bedroom.

There's a sofa that turns into a double bed against one wall, a small sink and compact units line the other. There's an electric radiator against the back wall and despite the size of it, the room is quite toasty. A door leads to a small shower and toilet, a very small space indeed, but it is our space for tonight.

'It's cute.'

'Small and cute enough for us to cosy up to each other,' Seb winked. 'Plus, I have a surprise for you.' He walked back out to the car and came back in with a cooler bag full of beer, and a bag full of food.

To the front of the hut there was a small in-ground fire pit and two chairs and Seb set about building a fire.

'We'll have some baked potatoes straight from the fire. How does that sound?'

'Sounds yummy.' I could barely wipe the smile from my face. I loved being away from home with Seb, just the two of us creating new memories on our little adventures.

Seb wrapped the potatoes in foil and threw them in the pit and we sat outside around the fire. He threw me a can of beer and then unwrapped a pack of tobacco and proceeded to roll himself a cigarette.

'Have a puff but take a long slow drag in and try not to let too much smoke out.'

'I don't smoke, you know that.'

'This is a different kind of cigarette; it will chill you out and make you feel amazing.' He nodded, looking at me expectantly.

I felt cornered and unable to refuse, so I took it between my lips and sucked it in. It tasted awful and I coughed and spluttered, but Seb encouraged me to try again.

One hour later we are talking about anything and everything, and nothing seemed to matter anymore. All my worries floated away with the smoke that escaped the fire as I listened to Seb talk about our future together.

TWENTY-NINE

Dani

As the months passed by I watched Laila settle back down and I was beyond thankful that she had ended her relationship with that horrible man. She had a new friend Alice who came over to the house once a week, and Laila spent time at hers, even sleeping over on the weekends. Sadly, she hadn't resolved her issues with Tayla but I hoped in time that they could put it behind them and be friends again.

I open up my email linked to my work article and I see a series of comments. Most of them are fine but there is one that stands out and is very direct and abusive. I am shocked that the paper has allowed it online and wonder about their screening system. It names me directly, not the pseudonym I use. *Round of applause. Maybe instead of crusading to save the world from your kitchen you should cherish your own family because you never know when it might be taken away from you.*

A wave of sickness ripples through me. I call the office and speak with my boss about screening comments that are posted and I try to reassure myself that there is nothing to worry about.

When I return home there is a note on the door saying I have some flowers to collect from my neighbour, Sally.

'Someone loves you,' she says as she hands a bouquet to me.

I thanked her and walked back into the house. I opened the card and read the words: *I thought you might be missing me.*

The card was blank so there was no way to track the shop that the flowers came from, but the I called the police and they told me to check my security cameras. When I logged on to my computer there was nothing but hazy black on the screen and when I walked outside to check them, the camera has been sprayed with black paint.

I raced next to door to Sally's and I knocked frantically on her door.

'Woah calm down, where's the fire?' She asked, confused at my agitated state.

Breathlessly I ask her, 'The person that delivered the flowers; what did they look like?'

'I don't know love. I had a knock on my door and when I answered the flowers were laid on my doorstep, and there was no one to be seen. Why is there a problem?'

'No. Nothing to worry about, there just wasn't a name on the card and I wondered who had sent them.' She looked at me strangely, so I made a quick exit to avoid any awkward questions.

Inside the house I felt on edge, so I arranged for someone to come and fit two new security cameras that were much more discreet. The new angle of the cameras meant I would be able to see whoever walked up the driveway. Hopefully the mystery person would be caught out if they came back.

'How was football?' I asked Chadd when he walked into the house.

'Good.' He replied as he opened the cupboard and grabbed a packet of cheese & onion crisps.

'Pizza tonight?'

'Sounds good. Chicken with extra chilli for me please.'

I quickly freshened myself up and jumped in the car. I picked up the half empty bottle of water that had been rolling around for the past week or so, annoying the hell out of me, and I placed it in the cup holder and made a mental note to clean the car during the week. It was just after five pm and there was still a lot of traffic on the road considering it was Saturday, and it seemed that everyone had decided to go to the same car park as me.

I was walking out of the supermarket when I bumped into Sarah, Alice's mum. I tried to rush past her so that I could get home before the food turned cold.

'Hi Sarah, as you can see, I'm like a pack horse here,' I laughed. 'We must have another catch up soon.'

'That would be lovely. Thanks for having Alice over last night. I'll be paying you board money soon!' She joked.

'I'm pretty sure it works out even. I hope the girls aren't too noisy for you tonight. Mind you, they aren't usually bad at all considering their age.'

I see her brow furrow in confusion.

'Tonight?' She queried.

'Yeah, Laila is sleeping at your house tonight, she left a couple of hours ago. That's what I meant when I said I'm sure it evens out, we have Alice on a Friday and you guys usually have Laila on a Saturday.'

Sarah was standing looking awkward and she kept pursing her mouth as if she'd forgotten how to speak.

'Are you OK, Sarah?' I asked.

She coughed awkwardly. 'There must have been some confusion I think because Alice is at her grandparent's house today. Liam and I are going to a friend's birthday this evening. That's why I'm here. I popped in to buy a gift.' She waved a bottle of champagne at me.

The bags of food suddenly become too heavy for my arms, and I try to gather my thoughts that have scattered like frightened birds.

'Can I ask if Laila stayed at your house two weekends ago on a Saturday night?'

'No, she didn't. I'm really sorry. Laila has only slept over at our house on two occasions. We've invited her to stay, but she said that she feels anxious when she sleeps away from home.'

I flushed red, aware that my daughter's deceit was now stood between us like a solid mass. I felt ashamed and naïve for trusting her.

'I'm sorry,' she said, genuinely, and I could see that she felt as awkward as I did about the situation.

'Does she have a boyfriend?' Sarah asked, and I felt my face reignite.

'No. Maybe I misunderstood her; she's probably staying at another friends. Sorry I'd better go; this pizza will be stone cold and her brother will not be impressed.'

I drive out onto the road in a daze and a car toots at me, making me jump. I feel as if everything is too bright and the traffic feels overwhelming. I can smell my own fear and all I want is to be home.

'What's up?' Chadd asks when I walk in. His brows are gathered together in concern and he looks so much like Luke. The ache of loss sits in my stomach. It will stay with me until the day I die.

'Do you know where your sister is?' My breath is short and gaspy.

'How would I know?' he seems puzzled. 'She's probably at Alice's house.'

'I've just bumped into her mum at the shopping centre and she's not there, where she is supposed to be.'

I call Laila's number and wait to see if she answers. I leave a voicemail, *Laila it's me. I don't know where you are, but I've got a good idea who you're with. I suggest that you get yourself home RIGHT NOW! You have an hour to ring me or come home, otherwise I will call the police.*

'I feel sick Chadd. If she has gone to this extreme to lie to us, what else is she doing? And what do we do if she doesn't call us?'

'I dunno.' he shrugged, looking genuinely worried.

'Do you know anything about this guy she's hanging out with?'

He shakes his head.

I watch the seconds on the clock tick by, aware that I will have no option but to phone the police if she does not come home soon.

THIRTY

Laila

Seb removed the potatoes from the fire to let them cool as we drank another beer. I was out of it with drinking and smoking weed. I felt so cool hanging out with him doing things like this. I forced myself off the floor, stumbled inside to the toilet and slipped off the seat banging my head on the door. I laughed out loud and Seb joined in from outside even though he had no idea what was funny.

'Will I put some music on?' I asked, as I scrolled through my phone.

We sang, ate, smoked, and drank some more and then we crashed into bed and my eyes closed before I hit the pillow.

I woke the next morning with a heartbeat in my head.

'Ouch,' I winced as I moved. 'What time is it?' My mouth was dry, and I staggered two steps from the bed to the sink. I turned the tap on filing up a glass, grateful for the cold water that slid down my throat. I downed two glasses before flopping back down on the bed. Seb was sat up, back against the wall with his eyes closed. 'You got a hangover?' he asked without looking at me.

'I guess. My head feels like it has its own heartbeat going on.'

'Yup, that's a hangover.'

'Have you seen my phone I need to know what time it is?' I asked.

'Nah, but we've got to be out of here for ten anyway so it can't be after that because they'd be knocking on the door. I had better get dressed and go clean up the mess from last night.'

Seb walked outside and I got dressed before joining him; daylight blinding me, making the ache behind my eyes pulse even harder. My phone was lying face down on the chair. I looked at the ground and took in the mess. Crumpled foil and a part baked potato lay next to a dozen or so empty cans of beer. Seb threw everything into a plastic bag without saying much, and I wondered if he was upset with me because I had flaked out last night.

'Will we do this again soon do you think? I had a great time.' I said, feeling slightly anxious.

'Maybe, we'll see.' He said nonchalantly.

I felt the butterflies take flight in my stomach. I had a sickly feeling that I had done something wrong.

We packed up quickly and got in the car to start making our way back home. I didn't want our night to end this way, I wanted to be going home happy and on cloud nine, not anxious and worried about us.

'Are we OK Seb?' I asked.

He looked at me and turned back to face the road, silence fell between us, and I swallowed down the lump that was rapidly growing in my throat.

'I'm not sure what the point of *us* is Laila. I mean, it's not like your mum is ever going to accept me into your family, and we can't keep sneaking around like this, it's costing me a fortune for fucks sake.' He snapped.

'I love you. Please Seb, I'm almost ready to leave school and then things will be different.'

'How?' he questioned angrily. 'How will they be different? *What* will be different exactly, because from what I see you aren't prepared to stand up to your family. You say you love me, yet you allow them to exclude me from your life.'

'It's not that easy. Mum's strict and what am I supposed to do? I have no money.'

'So grow some balls and tell your mum that we are together and that there's nothing she can do about it!'

He challenged me with a stare and the car momentarily swerved off the road and onto the grass verge sending my heart rate off the scale.

'I'll try,' I said quietly, feeling as if my life had just become way more complicated.

'Yeah, so you say.' He retorted, clearly disbelieving that I would.

'See ya,' he said, coldly when I stepped out of the car.

I walked slowly towards my house, the weight of my heartbreak consuming me. As I set foot on the drive the door swung open and suddenly there was noise and commotion.

'OH MY GOD, you're back!' My mum stumbled towards me and then started weeping and crying. I looked at her confused. My brother was running up to me. He hugged me while yelling about how worried he'd been. Gran was hugging mum and they were both crying. I followed them inside. A rock sat in my stomach.

'Where have you been Laila?' My mum asked, as she wiped tears from her face.

'You know where I've been. I've been to Alice's house,' I said, and I realized in that second that I've been busted.

'You have not! Do you know that we called the police and reported you as missing?'

Shit, this is bad.

'Did you even bother to check your phone?' Mum asked, her voice hoarse with emotion.

'I had no reception.'

'Oh really! And where were you to have *no reception?*'

'I, I ..' I can't bring myself to say the words and I stand there shuffling and looking at the floor. 'I'm sorry.'

'You were with him, weren't you?' Mum spat. I looked at her, it was crunch time. I could make a stand now or risk losing Seb, if I hadn't already.

'Yes I was with Seb.' I said, as I stared her in the eye, feeling far less brave than I probably looked.

Mum and gran start talking at the same time; mum about how I've deceived her, and gran about how the police were out looking for me.

'I hope you know that you will not be going anywhere again for a very long time. We will take you to and from school, you're not having any sleepovers, or library visits after school, unless we are with you. Got it?'

Seb was right, my mum was the only thing coming between us, and she were determined to split us up.

'Well maybe if you weren't so stuck in the dark ages, I wouldn't have had to lie!' I yelled, and for the first time in my life, my mother slapped me across the cheek, shocking me into silence. I stared at her and I could see that she was just as shocked as I was. She reached out and I stepped away from her.

'Laila I am so sorry,' she sobbed, before breaking down and crying again.

'So as well as being ridiculously strict you're now abusing me!' I shouted before running up the stairs.

'Laila, no! Don't be so silly, it was an accident, my nerves are so fraught, I, I lost control for a second that's all. I've been so worried about you and haven't slept a wink all night.' She shouted up after me

'I wonder what your boss would think if she knew that you hit your own daughter?' I yelled from the top of the stairs. She stepped backwards as if the words had physically hit her. 'Maybe I could call your boss and they could write an article about child abuse,' I added.

I walked into my room and slammed the door. There was no going back now.

THIRTY-ONE

Laila

Life had been a nightmare since the overnight event. Mum had taken my mobile phone and my IPad from me, and she drove me to and from school which was super embarrassing. The only time I was allowed my laptop was when I was doing homework and I had to sit at the table and she basically watched my every move. It was child abuse as far as I was concerned. My loathing for her grew daily.

I hated not being able to speak to Seb or see him. I had no way of letting him know anything. The last time I had spoken to him was when I'd returned home from our night away, and my mum forced me to call him and say it was over.

I wrote poetry at night to help get out how I felt. I wished I had an address to post it to Seb, but one day I would show him and he would understand how much I loved him.

YOU

Each second of each day,

I lie awake and pray,

That I will soon be in your arms,

Wrapped in love, safe from harm.

The ache I feel inside my heart,

Is making me feel weak,

I close my eyes and see your face,

I long for us to speak.

My life is empty without you,
I search, but I am lost,
We will be together soon,
Regardless of the cost.

I woke early on Monday to the smell of toast and the clatter of a dish hitting marble. Chadd never had been able to place his bowl of cereal down gently.

I ate breakfast, ignoring my mother who chuntered on in the background, trying to engage me in conversation as if nothing had happened.

'Maybe I could get a movie tonight, Laila. What do you think?'

'I *think* that I would rather read a book, thanks all the same.'

'For goodness' sake we have been over this.' She sighed. 'Seb is too old and he's not good for you.'

'Can I go to school now?' I asked. I couldn't listen to another Seb slating session, so I made a quick exit.

We drove the ten-minute trip to school in silence.

During lunch break I gave Alice some money to go to the tuck shop and buy us some snacks. I told her that I would look after her bag and wait for her under the tree. As soon as she left, I took her mobile out and punched in Seb's number.

'Seb, it's me.'

'You've got a new phone?'

'No, I'm calling from Alice's phone, so I won't have long. I miss you. I hate this.'

'Me too.'

Silence filled the distance between us. 'Are we still OK?" I asked tentatively.

'I thought we were done Lai. Your mum won't let you out of the house, so how can there be an *us*.'

'Don't say that Seb, I love you. All I want is to be with you.'

'Prove it then.' He threw the challenge out like an anchor, making me stop in my tracks.

'How? I can't go anywhere.'

'You can leave home. And because you're sixteen no one can make you go back.'

The breath left my body as the enormity of his words hit like a freight train.

'You want me to leave home?' I asked, my head spinning with fear.

'Well, if you love me, you will. Simple. Think about it and call me back in a couple of days. Don't leave me hanging around for too long though Laila. The decision lies with you as to where we go from here.' He ended the call and I stood numb before I slipped the phone back into Alice's bag. I walked towards Alice who was clearly looking for me.

'There you are,' she said looking confused. 'Where have you been?'

'I thought you would be queuing up for a while, so I went for a wander.' I lied.

'Here's your food.' She handed it to me, and I put it in my bag, my appetite had vanished after my conversation with Seb.

Alice clicked her fingers in front of my face.

'Hey, you still with me? You're acting weird, are you alright?'

'Yeah, I just feel a bit unwell actually.' I said, and for once I was telling the truth.

That night I lay on my bed and Seb's words swirled around and around my head. I tried to picture what my life might look like if I left home, and my insides tightened as if being squeezed by an invisible hand. It was pretty hard to imagine a life that you've never had. I thought about waking up next to Seb and eating breakfast, watching movies together and sharing private jokes. I imagined my life without him, and I felt sick.

The following day at school I begged Alice to let me log into my Facebook account.

'What evs, just don't use all of my credit.' She said.

The first thing I did was check Seb's page. His last status read: : *When people treat you like they don't care, believe them.*

Oh god, he was feeling that I didn't care.

'Can I quickly call my mum, Alice?' I asked.

'Yeah sure.' She walked off giving me some privacy.

'Seb, it's me. Can you email me? I need to know what your plans are if I leave home.'

'Why, You'll not do it anyway.' He challenged.

'Don't say that. What you're asking is huge. Email me and then I'll reply as soon as I can.'

That night I ate dinner and then I asked if I could have the laptop to finish my assignment. Mum checked that I was writing and then sat down to watch TV. I sat at the back of the dining table, so I had time to click out of email if she came to check on me.

I opened my email and clicked on Seb's name. I read the message he had sent.

Hi Laila. Miss ya. Look I'm not sure what you want me to say to be honest. All I know is that I'm getting such mixed messages from you. You tell me that you love me then you choose to stay away from me. I feel as if you're messing me around. Your family will never accept me – unless you make a stand. I guess I'm waiting now to see what you will do. If you're willing to stand up to your mum then I suggest we leave, I'm not sure you love me enough for that though. Time will tell.

If you don't come with me, we will be over. I can't let you hurt me like this any longer. You have two days to decide.

Seb.

He truly thought that I didn't care. I really had no option but to go, otherwise I would lose him.

As soon as I had made the decision to leave home adrenalin kicked in and it felt like an exciting adventure. I made excuses to leave the homework and I went upstairs and took my small suitcase from under my bed. I grabbed a bar of soap and some shampoo from the landing cupboard. My mother was a compulsive hoarder. She had to have three of everything, and when there was a sale on you could guarantee double that. I started laying out my clothes to see what I would take with me. I had no idea how long I would be gone but I hoped one week would be enough to make mum see that she couldn't force us to stay away from each other. I couldn't wait. It would be so nice not having anyone tell me what to do. I pictured myself being dropped off at school by Seb in the mornings and seeing the envy in everyone's faces. They would be *so* jealous that I was living with my boyfriend.

The day before I was leaving it was mum's birthday, and when I got home from school she surprised me with a manicure.

'I thought we could maybe go to the theatre in a few weeks or to a music concert. What do you think?' Mum asked as we sat with our feet soaking in a plastic bowl; the overpowering smell of nail varnish stinging our eyes. I could barely look her in the eye.

'Maybe.' I mumbled.

That night we went out to an Italian restaurant. Gran and Peter had travelled from Wales, and they were already waiting at the table. Gran had flown Elanor over from Spain as a surprise and I was pleased because mum would need her when I had gone.

We had a meal and one of the staff came out with a birthday cake for mum and everyone started singing happy birthday to her. She blushed and laughed and for a second she looked young and happy. Guilt slammed me in the throat as I looked around the table.

The morning of my escape arrived and the plan was that I would go to school as normal and then after lunch I would say that I had vomited. I played out the part well by going straight to bed after mum's birthday meal saying that I felt unwell and maybe I had eaten too much.

Thirty minutes before lunch I left the classroom, and I told the admin staff that I had been sick. They rang my mum who came to pick me up, and ironically I did feel sick and I looked pale, but that was the anxiety at the thought of carrying out this plan.

'I will have to call your gran and see if she can some and sit with you. I have a meeting this afternoon that I can't get out of.'

'Mum, please, I am sixteen I don't need a babysitter.' She reluctantly agreed to leave me as long as I stayed in bed and called her if I needed anything. I could see she was hesitant.

I gave her twenty minutes and then I called her to say I was in bed and going to sleep and that if I needed anything I would call gran.

I rang Seb from the house phone and arranged for him to pick me up in thirty minutes. I took some food out of the cupboard and made sure that I had clothes, shoes, a coat and some money that I had been saving for a while. I left the house and walked to where Seb was waiting. It was early May and flower buds were starting to bloom and the smell of summer was within reach.

I put my suitcase in the boot and stepped into Seb's car.

'My god Laila, I never thought that you would do it. I truly did not think that you would go through with it.' Seb's smile spread from one ear to the other and I had never seen him look so happy.

'Where are we going?'

'Just wait and see. You're gona love it Lai, it will be our little love nest.' I blushed and sat back sighing. I felt so happy right now. Seb was right, all that mattered was us being together. 'Here's the new phone I promised you.' He handed me a box with a Samsung 9s. I couldn't' stop squealing with excitement.

We drove for hours, and I closed my eyes, waking when the last sun of the day had almost dissolved behind the clouds. 'Where are we?' I asked, not recognizing our surroundings.

'Wait and see,' Seb replied, as he drove into an industrial estate and got out of the car. He took something out of the boot and disappeared. When he returned, he was smiling to himself before he spun the car around and reversed. I started to feel slightly panicked and I had no idea why.

'What's happening?' Seb looked at me and winked. The next thing I knew he was out of the car, and I turned around and saw him hooking his car up to a small caravan. 'Welcome to Wales baby, and happy new home,' he said, as we drove off towing the caravan behind us.

My stomach sank and the bubble burst as reality hit me. I had now officially left home and suddenly it didn't feel so exciting anymore.

THIRTY-TWO

Laila

We pulled up on a side road off from the motorway and Seb told me to get out of the car. I couldn't believe that we were sleeping on a roadside. He opened the door to the caravan and a smell of damp hit me as I scrutinized the interior. Seats framed the window on three sides leaving a very small, carpeted space in between. The sofa cushions were grubby with worn patches peppered across them; the fabric all but disintegrated. The carpet, once beige, was now a splattered mix of stains. The net curtains that hung had some sort of dirt or fungi growing from the bottom upwards giving the impression they'd been dip dyed. There was a small sink area with kettle, toaster and a few cupboards with sticky plastic covering that was peeling away at the edges. I opened the door to the bathroom. A shower, toilet and sink all fit snuggly into the tiny space and it had been a long time since any of them had been cleaned. I felt quite sick.

'So, we are in Wales, right?' I queried.

'Yep, rainy Wales, where the hills are green, and language is in a world of it's own.'

'I'm just wondering how I'm going to get to school from here?'

Seb looked stunned, and then he burst out laughing. In fact, he was doubled up, a deep belly laugh which crinkled the side of his eyes. I smiled, unsure of what was funny, but Seb's laughter was contagious.

He stopped suddenly, his expression changing. 'You didn't seriously think I was going to drive you to school every day, did you? I'm not your fucking father.'

My face burned and I opened my mouth to speak, but I had nothing to say, so I just sat with my embarrassment. My mind was whirling and the enormity of what I have done hit me. I burst out crying. I think about my family, frantic with worry about where I am and who I am with, and I feel ill. I wish that I could turn the clock back to before I had agreed to this. I misunderstood the whole thing and thought that I would still be living life as I always had, with the exception that I would be living with Seb. Anxiety welled up in me with such force it knocked the breath out of me leaving me gasping for air. I felt lost as I looked around this filthy caravan; it was so far removed from what I had imagined life would be like. I was already missing my warm house, the internet, and a nice clean bath to lie in.

'I've made a lot of sacrifices to get us this caravan Laila, I hope you're not going to start complaining and crying on like a baby.' Seb said. He was pissed off, I could tell the way he was looking at me, and suddenly the space in the caravan felt even smaller.

'It's just, I just assumed I would be going to school, I haven't even sat my exams yet. My mum will kill me if I leave school without any qualifications.'

'Jesus, Laila! Start acting like the adult you say you want to be. You're acting like a spoilt fucking child. You can get a job, who needs crappy qualifications anyway? Come on lighten up, this is supposed to be an adventure. Remember this is all your mother's fault. If she'd been cool with us, we wouldn't be here right now.' He stared at me.

'You're right,' I said, swallowing down my anxiety as I set about cleaning with what few products there were underneath the kitchen unit.

Five days has passed since I left home. Every day we move on to a new place so not to draw attention to ourselves. Thankfully, Seb had agreed that we could stay on a campsite for a few days. I was desperate to have a real shower and explore the area.

'You can't go wandering around like you're on fucking holiday. Your mum will
have reported you missing so you'll have to stay inside.'

'I need to shower and wash clothes.'

'Do you have to whine like a dog? Go and get a shower and make sure you speak
to no one and wear a hat or pull your hood up. Whatever you do, do not draw
attention to yourself. Got it?'

Once I had showered and put our clothes in the washing machine, Seb and I
went for a walk. I had a jacket on and my hood up so no one could see my face.
We walked out of the caravan site and into the thick of the trees that lined the
riverbank. Damp leaves spattered the ground and the smell of woodsmoke drifted
across the river as we walked, making my stomach rumble. I thought of mum's
roast beef dinners, and I wished I was sat at the dining room table eating with
my family. I straddled a tree trunk that was sticking out over the river and Seb
sat beside me, but apart. I watched the river gently follow its path over stones and
rocks as the moon shone onto the water. It felt good to be outside breathing fresh
air rather than the stale rot of that caravan we were staying in.

We walked back to the caravan after an hour, and we ate beans on toast in
silence. There was no TV so we played some music which I was thankful for
because the silence was smothering me.

The following morning after a restless night, Seb dropped the bombshell that
he was going back home to do some work. I asked him if I could go with him but
he shut that down straight away. Part of me longed for breathing space from him
because he had been so moody since we left. He would ignore me for hours and
he kept disappearing to talk on his phone, only he would never tell me who he
was talking to. I asked to call my mum, to let her know that I was safe, and he
flipped out. I tried to reason with him and make him see how worried she would
be but he raged on about this being her fault, pacing back and forward. It took
him so long to calm down that I was now too scared to mention it again.

I felt trapped now; devastated that I was causing my family so much worry, but
too scared to return because I would be in so much trouble. And in amongst it
all was my love for Seb.

THIRTY-THREE

Dani

I opened the front door quietly, hoping that Laila was still sleeping off her sickness. I put the kettle on and note the clean kitchen and sink free of dishes. She'd not eaten. I gently knocked on her door before opening it.

'Lail-,' I whispered, and stopped. My heart started thumping erratically. She wasn't in her room and her bed was made up. I ran around the house checking all rooms and there was no sign of her. I called her mobile and it trilled away in my bedside cabinet. I cursed myself for having taken it from her. I opened the wardrobe and sank to my knees. Her clothes were gone, and her suitcase was gone from under her bed. Laila had run away from home.

I floundered around the house like a fish out of water, not knowing which way to turn. Mum and Elanor rushed through the door as I sat with my head in my hands.

'What do I do?' I asked, desperately. 'I've called Alice and she hasn't heard from Laila. She's still not talking to Tayla and the other girls so she's not with them.'

'She's gone from model child to child from hell in the space of a few months.' Mum said, sadness evident in her eyes.

'You need to call the police,' Elanor said firmly. I nodded, thankful that someone was able to give me some basic instructions because I was numb.

One hour later two police officers arrived and fired a list of questions at me.

'How long has she been in a relationship with this man?' The young officer asked.

'Well, that's sort of complicated. They were in a relationship earlier in the year but I disapproved of it so we told her to end it.' I flushed, feeling shame creep over me.

'How old is this man that she is with?'

'Laila told us that he's eighteen, but he looks older. Maybe early twenties?'

'And what's his name?' The female asked. 'We only know his first name. It's Sebastian.' I felt myself turn red again and I can't look at them. An awkward silence sits between us.

'Do you happen to have a photograph of them together?' Again, my skin prickled with shame. 'No, I don't sorry. We only ever met him once or twice so it's hard to remember what he looked like, other than him having dark hair. I think he has a tattoo on his arm, some tribal kind of tattoo from his shoulder part way down top of his arm.' I said, hoping that my small snippet of information might be enough to help. 'I've seen his car, it's a black sporty kind, like a racer car.'

'Do you think your daughter has been taken against her will?

'No. I don't know!' The question makes me want to shout yes from the top of my lungs, but deep down I know this was planned. The feigned sickness was all part of the plot to get her home, and it made sense her now being so defensive about her gran coming to look after her. 'I've got her phone. She's bound to have a photo on there of the two of them,' I say, feeling hopeful.

I open the screen but it asks for a password. I try a few basic ones and realize I haven't a clue what Laila would use as a password because she is a stranger to me.

'I can't access anything because I don't know her password.' I say.

'We can arrange for an IT specialist to look at the phone with your permission. Hopefully there will be photograph of the two of them.'

'OK. Thank you. Is there anything else I can be doing?' I ask.

'Just make sure you keep your phone charged in case Laila calls you.' The officer suggested before leaving.

I sit down and put my head in my hands, lost in a world that suddenly feels familiar, a feeling that belongs to a past life. Everything I thought I was certain of is made of smoke and no longer feels tangible.

'I will stay with you until Laila comes home, Dani,' Elanor says, and I thank my lucky stars that amongst the chaos, she is always there like a tower of strength for me.

It had been five days since my baby girl had gone missing and so far, there had been no sightings of her. I couldn't sleep, I couldn't eat, and I had constant anxiety. Not to mention the flashbacks I was having as my mind ran crazy. I had managed to assist the police artist to create an E-fit of what Seb looked like, and that had been televised. I'd not had much luck with his car though because all I could remember was that it was dark and sporty looking.

Two days later I received a delivery on my doorstep. A wreath, with a card and the words: *Sorry for the loss of your loved one. I hope your days ahead are not too painful. From someone who understands your pain.*

I screamed a blood-curdling scream and fell to the floor. Chadd and Elanor came running down the stairs.

'Dani what's wrong?' I couldn't answer because sobs were bursting from my chest like an overflowing river. Elanor looked at the flowers and picked the card up that lay on the floor.

'I don't understand.'

'Nor do I.' I wept.

I felt as if I had no control over my life anymore. My daughter was missing and I had no idea where she was. We were all clinging to a thread, unable to hold ourselves together and therefore unable to support each other. My nights were almost void of sleep, weighed down by guilt and feelings of failure. I felt embarrassed that my daughter had run away from home with an older man. I wished that I didn't, but I did. I felt as if everyone else was thinking the same, *fancy her daughter taking off with an older man, there must be more to the story than meets the eye.* It was easier not to face people, so we hid behind the bricks of what had always been our safe haven.

I took the flowers and card into the police station and then called to the supermarket because we were almost out of food. I grabbed a trolley and walked quickly to the fruit and veg section, throwing in whatever I could so that I could make my escape as fast as possible. I could feel eyes burning through me, staring, as people talked in hushed voices about my family situation, only they don't talk quietly enough and I can catch odd words floating through the air like butterflies. *Daughter, missing, boyfriend, problems.* I push my trolley faster as my breathing escalated, creating a feeling of panic inside of me. I grabbed at bread, snacks, and tins of food that can be reheated and I realized that I have forgotten to buy meat. I walk back shakily toward the chilled meat section and as I turn the corner, I see one of the school mums gossiping to a woman I've not seen before. She turned as if having detected me and flushes slightly which tells me that she has most likely been having a good old bitch about my family. I try to avoid her and wheel the trolley the other way, but she makes a beeline for me calling out my name.

'Dani how are you, poor darling? I was going to call, but ...' the unsaid words hung in the air. 'You know how it is.' She smiled awkwardly, waiting for me to speak. I started putting packs of different meat into the trolley not really focusing on what I was buying.

'I have to go, sorry,' I said in a bid to get away from her and her poisonous tongue. Her hand reached out and grabbed my shoulder.

'Any news Dani? Have you found out where she is yet or who she is with?'

I was so tempted to make up a story on the spot to shut her up; standing there looking at me with her fake sincerity, when really all she would do is take any information I gave her and run her mouth off. I shook my head as tears threatened to fall, and I pushed my trolley away as fast as I could to the echos of her shouting "call me if you need anything".

Like hell I thought.

THIRTY-FOUR

Laila

It was day nine of us living together. Seb was starting to complain about how much fuel was costing because of the amount of moving around we were doing. He preferred to park along a deserted roadside on a small plot of land, which meant no electricity. Our diet consisted mostly of cheap noodles and bags of crisps, and I was missing my home comforts more than I'd ever thought I would. I longed to be able to curl up on the sofa and watch TV. I dreamt about lying on my comfortable bed with fresh bedding, listening to music with the heating on. I missed cupboards full of food that I usually complained about, and I realized that I had behaved like a spoilt little brat for years. I had no credit on my phone and I missed my mum's voice. I even missed my brother way more than I thought I would.

I watched Seb out of the window and wondered who he was talking to. Eventually he came inside, bringing with him the mud from the patchy, rain-soaked grass. and I watched him walk across the small carpet area, leaving boot prints on the already stained carpet. The smell of wet earth hung heavy in the air. In my head I pictured my mum's response to someone walking into the house and leaving mud everywhere. I realized I was thinking a lot about my mum lately.

'I'm going away in a hour, you know the job I mentioned.'

I looked at him wide eyed and opened my mouth to speak. I had no recollection of him mentioning a job.

'What's up are you scared? Do you want your mommy?' He mocked.

'Don't be stupid,' I said defensively. 'It's just that I've never spent a night all alone before.'

'Don't worry, I'll take you back to the caravan park so there'll be other people around.'

We drove to the nearest caravan park which was in Llanrwst, a word I could not pronounce. The park was situated on the outskirts of the market village and set amongst the lushest, greenest grass, I had ever seen.

'What time will you be back tomorrow do you think?' I asked, desperate to keep the fear out of my voice.

'Probably be late, maybe eight pm, depending on traffic.'

'Seb what will we do long term? We can't keep travelling from place to place like this. Money is a problem, and you say I'm too young to work. Should we not just go home?' I couldn't help but test the waters even though I was terrified about what his reaction might be.

He stopped what he was doing and spun to face me.

'So, you want to go home do you?' It was a question that came out more like a statement. 'You want to go back to being grounded and locked in your bedroom by your controlling fucking mother, not allowed to have an opinion of your own or make choices of your own. Is that what you want? For us to be apart again, because if it is say now and I'll fucking drive you straight back to your brick jail house!' He was almost snorting steam from his nostrils and my heart lurched in fear.

'No, no, that's not what I want, it's just that I can't really leave the caravan either so I feel as if I've swapped one prison for another.' The words came out of my mouth without my consent.

Seb walked towards me, globules of spit flying as he spoke.

'Being with me is prison is it princess?' He sneered, and I felt too scared to respond. 'Well pack your fucking bags then and you can fuck off home!' He yelled. 'Go on! Off you fuck!'

An elderly woman popped her head out of the caravan next to us. 'Is everything okay in there?' She asked before Seb quickly closed the door.

'I'm sorry, please Seb, I just want us to be happy and I guess what I imagined is very different to the reality, that's all. Of course I want to be with you,' I said the words but wasn't feeling certain that I did anymore.

Seb pushed me onto the makeshift bed and started kissing my neck. I was confused but went along with it, relieved that our fight would be over. It was different this time though, almost as if he was still angry when he was supposed to be making love to me. He stood up afterwards, zipped his jeans up and walked to the door.

'I'll be back tomorrow. Don't leave the caravan and don't talk to anyone.' With that, he slammed the door and drove off leaving me feeling confused and very emotional.

I paced the floor wondering what I could do and after an hour of almost going crazy I decided to go for a walk. I wandered to the site office and picked up a few leaflets and asked the way to the town. It was around a fifteen-minute walk along the riverbank and over a bridge. It was so picturesque. I walked with the sound of the river accompanying me and the swans that floated along gracefully, like royalty. Over the bridge a solid brick house sat at one end, covered in ivy that had grown all over the front of the house, including the roof. I felt a yearning to knock on the door and go inside, but I kept on walking until I reached the town centre.

Market stalls lined either side of the central space with shops lining the streets as far as the eye could see. I popped into a local souvenir shop and examined all of the items on show. I took a shine to a key ring that had a picture of a red dragon on and I picked it up and slipped it into my pocket. I had never stolen anything in my life, but I only had five pounds and I wanted to keep that for food. I was sick of eating noodles and cheese sandwiches, so I was going to go to a bakery and buy myself a pie. I would tell Seb that I'd lost the money.

I spent two hours walking around all of the shops before I made my way back to the caravan park. I stopped on the way and sat along the riverbank with my back against a tree and I ate my food, savouring every mouthful. It made me think about homeless people and my heart ached for them.

I listened to the water trickle past me. It felt so peaceful and for a second I forgot that I was a missing person, I was just someone on holiday enjoying the sights and sounds around them. I walked slowly back to the entrance of the caravan park, reluctant to step inside the damp, dirty, caravan that I was now calling home.

As I neared the door the old lady from the van opposite came out.

'Hello dear, have you just arrived?' I nodded. 'I wondered if you would like a cup of tea, I'm feeling a bit lonely. My husband has gone for a walk with the dog and my legs aren't what they used to be, so I have to spend a lot of time indoors.' She seemed so sweet, and I was craving company.

'OK,' I smiled. It wouldn't do any harm to talk to her and I was so bored of my own company.

'So how long are you staying?' She asked, once I was seated. Her caravan smelled like furniture polish, and it reminded me of my gran's house. The carpets were clean and the beige sofa looked so comfortable and inviting next to the fire place. On a small side table next to a lamp, there was a game of monopoly and scrabble, and a pack of playing cards.

'Oh, I'm not sure just a night or two.' I smiled.

She nodded, and smiled as she filled the kettle and switched it on, before placing two china cups and matching saucers on the bench.

'What's your name honey? Mine is Millie.'

I faltered before replying. 'Alice. My name is Alice.' I had no idea why I had given that name, it had just been the first one that popped in my head.

Millie poured some tea in the pot and sat it on the table that was directly opposite the kitchen. She took out a packet of chocolate digestives and handed my one.

'Tell me about your travels Miss Alice, I love to hear people's stories. My husband and I are here for two weeks. We come every year and have since our kids were young.' Millie said before offering another biscuit. She goes on to tell me that she has two daughters, one son, six grandchildren and one great grandchild. She used to work in a factory and her husband was a mechanic with his own business, but they are retired now.

'What brings you to Wales?' She asked gently, and her voice is like a lullaby to my ears, soft, gentle, and hypnotic.

'Ah, just on holiday for a week that's all.' I said, trying to avoid eye contact with her.

'With your brother?' She probed.

'Err. Yeah, my brother.'

'You seem awfully young Alice. Should you not be in school?'

I looked at her and start to feel under pressure.

'I take one week off a year; my brother is in the army and I don't see him much.' I said quickly.

'I see,' she said, looking at me kindly. 'He seemed a little angry this morning and I noticed that his car is gone now.'

'Yeah, he's fine, bad sleep with the post-traumatic stress that's all.' I said, impressed with myself and thankful for all of the Netflix I had watched while I was at home. 'I better be going back now because he'll be home soon. Thank you for the tea and biscuits, it was so nice to meet you.' I stand to make a quick exit.

'Take some magazines with you Alice, I'm finished with them.' She handed me two and gave me a brief hug.

Thanks, that's really kind of you.'

'You're welcome, dear, thank you for keeping an old lady company.' I closed the door behind me and walked back into my prison walls, walls that felt even more claustrophobic after being in Millie's van.

Later that night I woke with a start as the door closed. It was pitch black because the tea-light candles had burnt out.

'Fuck that hurt,' Seb said as he walked into the kitchen cupboard. I sat up and rubbed my eyes. Seb crashed out next to me and the next time I opened my eyes daylight was forcing its way through the thin curtains.

'You can't beat the smell of bacon cooking in a caravan don't you think?' Seb asked a short while later. I looked at the blackened pan he was cooking the bacon in and my stomach constricted. No matter how hard I tried, all I could see was filth around me, whereas Seb looked quite comfortable in this environment.

'Did your parents have a caravan?' I asked him, curious to know more about his background.

'No doubt you would have been overseas to Spain and places like that on your holidays?' He queried, while completely avoiding my question. I tried to read his mood, because yet again he'd switched from happy to angry without any provocation. I decide it's best not to answer.

We eat in silence, my stomach struggling to hold on to the food. While washing the dishes Seb picks up of the magazines that Millie gave me.

'Where the fuck did these come from?'

'The old woman over there gave them to me.' I point at her van.

Seb grabbed me around the throat.

'What did I tell you, you stupid little bitch. I told you to stay inside and not speak to anyone!'

I started crying and he let go of me and walked out of the van, slamming the door behind him, causing the frame to shake.

I look out of the window and Millie is poking her head from behind the curtains.

'What you looking at you nosy old cow?' Seb snarled.

'Get packed up.' Seb ordered as he walked back in. 'We'll have to move because you can't even follow simple instructions! You're just like your mother poking your fucking nose into people's business when it doesn't concern you.'

I had no idea what Seb was ranting on about so I stayed silent and made sure that everything was locked up in the caravan.

'Alice, are you alright, dear?' Millie asked, as I locked the caravan. I nodded and smiled.

'Congrats on fucking up our plan Laila.' Seb said as we pulled out of the caravan site. 'I thought you were mature enough to handle this but seems I was wrong.'

We drove in silence and pulled over on some old waste ground not long before the sun went down. Seb had stopped at a supermarket along the way and bought booze, tobacco, beans, and noodles. I looked at our setting. The food. I felt a heaviness settle within me.

Seb handed me a beer.

I drank down the beer, enjoying the way it unknotted my muscles and dissolved some of the heaviness in my chest.

'You understand why I was angry?' He questioned. 'What if she calls the police? That means they know what we are and that we are also towing a caravan. That makes us easy targets.'

'She was just a nice old lady that was lonely that's all.'

'Maybe, but we can't take any risks.'

He's calmer now. He goes into his pocket and brings out a chunk of brown stuff and sniffs it. 'It's my chill pill babe.' He said and smiled a smile that first melted my heart. 'Want some?'

I felt as if I'd made enough childish mistakes for one day, so keen to gain back some kind of street cred I nodded.

I inhaled the smoke, choking less this time than I did the first. I feel relief as my body starts to relax and let go of the tension I am holding, and I swallow down the questions that surface in my mind about what lies ahead of us.

THIRTY-FIVE

Laila

Our new location was Holyhead, a large town with a very busy port in North-western Wales. We arrived just after one pm and sat in a chip shop at the port watching the hustle and bustle of men offloading their catch of the day before heading back out to sea. The noxious smell of fish was overpowering and the screams of herring gulls almost drowned out the television that played in the background.

My eyes were glued to the TV, having missed the comfort of it over the past two weeks, when suddenly a picture of Seb and I flashed up on the screen. I froze, unsure if I should stay put and watch, or run. I looked to Seb to see what his reaction was and instead of looking fearful he was intently watching the screen, smiling to himself.

'What do we do now? Should we not leave here?' I asked.

'Now is when the fun begins baby.' He said, wearing an expression that I'd not seen before. I suddenly felt scared and I had no idea why. I considered walking up to someone and saying that I needed help but then Seb put his arm around my back and and walked me to the car.

'What did you mean now the fun begins?' I probed.

'Well the police have a description, so now things will get exciting. The first thing I will need is a new car. That means we might have to ditch the caravan and just buy a tent, but your bitch of a mother will not be getting you back anytime soon.'

My stomach flipped. I hated it when Seb spoke about my mum like that.

'Why do you hate my mum so much?'

'You'll find out in your own good time. Imagine how worried your mum must be. She'll be wondering if she's ever going to see you again and that must feel weird for her, especially after losing your dad.' He was smiling to himself again and it was freaking me out. 'She'll be crying every day feeling as if her heart's been ripped out, her anxiety levels will be through the roof and she's probably not eating because she'll be so stressed out.'

'You seem pretty happy about that.'

'Hell yeah,' he said as he walked into a camping store to buy a tent. 'Wait next to the car and pull the hood over your head.'

I walked to the car, eyes down, head to the ground. Part of me wanted to run away from Seb because he was acting odd and I didn't like it, and the other part of me wanted to hang on to the Seb that I knew and loved. The car boot opened causing me to jump.

We drove away from Holyhead along the winding lanes that were lined with trees. I thought about home, and mum, Chadd, Gran, Peter, and Elanor, and the things that Seb had said. I pictured mum crying on the sofa looking at pictures of me when I was younger, and I wondered how I had ended up in this situation. It had all seemed to happen so fast and I'd not thought through the consequences of my actions. Once minute a guy was whistling at me outside of school, the next I'd ran away from home! I couldn't ever picture walking back into my house without there being lots of aggro. I felt so ashamed of what I'd done. Seb would be in so much trouble, and it all just felt so overwhelming.

I closed my eyes and drifted off to sleep, dreaming that I was back home in my bedroom. Chadd was playing his Xbox too loud, so I shout at him to turn it down. I wake with my heart racing and thoughts of my big brother at the forefront of my mind.

Seb steered the car towards an open field and kept driving.

'What are you doing?' I asked, panic stricken.

'We're setting up home babe.'

I looked all around us. There was nothing but rolling hills for miles around, no shelter, no toilet facilities, just grass and lots of it.

'Where?'

'Just over there,' He said, pointing to an opening near some trees.

'We're camping on moors?' I asked incredulously.

'We sure are. Need to drag this out as long as possible babe. Make sure your mum gets the message and there's less chance of the police finding us here. If we go to a camp site we are easy targets now that our faces are spread across the news.'

One hour later Seb has erected the tent and built a makeshift firepit. We had a gas stove to cook on and two lanterns.

'Where's the toilet?' I asked.

'Right that way.' Seb pointed towards the dense forest area.

'There's a toilet in there? In the middle of nowhere?'

'There's a toilet wherever you dig one.' He handed me a metal shovel and I stormed back to the car and sat in the passenger seat and cried. Seb walked to the car and quickly opened the door.

'What's wrong princess? Is this not good enough for you?' He pushed me and I recoiled in fear. He started ranting and I was terrified of the person that he had turned into. I no longer knew who he was.

'Do you know the sacrifices I have made for you? I am a wanted man and it's all your fault!' He said, as he gripped my neck with his hand. I panicked and automatically tried to get his hand off my throat but that only made him grip harder. 'You are nothing but an ungrateful little bitch!' He spat at me.

'Please Seb, stop.' I managed to whisper through his grip on my windpipe. He let go and stared at me and I waited for him to speak, too afraid of angering him further by saying the wrong thing.

'I don't know what you want from me Laila. It's like whatever I do is just not fucking good enough for you. You're definitely your mother's daughter that's for sure, judging me, and always fucking complaining. Do this, do fucking that.'

Seb continued to rant on, and half of what he was saying made no sense whatsoever. I was scared and it was cutting in dark now as the sun fell from the sky, causing shadows to look out from the forest, and birds to scatter from trees. I was afraid of staying in this isolated place with him when he was behaving this way and I regretted not acting on my earlier instincts to get help. Now I was stuck here with no way of finding anyone. We had driven for miles and I had no clue where we were.

'Are you even FUCKING listening to me? Get out of the car', he ordered. I did as I was told and to my horror he jumped into the driver's seat, turned the engine on and drove off. I chased the car but couldn't keep up.

'Seb, No! Don't leave me here on my own. I'm sorry, please!' I screamed, and cried, but he just kept driving slow enough to be able to see my desperation, but fast enough so that I could not catch up with him. He sped up once he reached the top of the hill and I sunk to the ground. I wanted my mum and I didn't even have any way of getting in touch with her. I walked back towards the tent and sat waiting for him to come back. I retraced the whole scenario from the beginning and still couldn't comprehend how it had ended like this. I had been upset about the lack of facilities but surely that wasn't enough to warrant him going off like that.

I had no battery on the mobile that Seb had given me so I had no idea what time it was or how long it had been since he had driven off. There were noises coming from the forest that had my heart pumping like a steam train and I felt so vulnerable in this tent all alone in the dark. The lanterns only gave off enough glow to see directly around me and Seb had the lighter so I couldn't even light the fire that he had prepared. The trees groaned and creaked as the wind whipped through them, and occasionally there was the sound of rustling, which made me shake with fear as I pictured foxes or other wild animals sniffing around outside. I sobbed and sobbed and I desperately needed to go to the toilet for a pee but I was now too scared to go. I felt as if the forest had come alive and I was trapped in a living horror movie that I had not agreed to be a part of. I peed next to the tent, shame washing over me as reality hit home that I had truly made the biggest mistake of my life. It made me think of a storybook that had belonged to my dad. I had found it one day in the attic and read all of the stories. Hansel and Gretel had stuck with me, giving me nightmares because I remembered feeling terrified at the thought of two children being lost in a forest. I felt as if that childhood fear had actually come true, only I was alone, and not with my brother.

I thought I might die of stress during the night. My breathing was tight and laboured and I felt detached from my body. I was heartbroken that Seb had left me here all alone in the dark in the middle of a field, with no way of getting in touch with anyone and I was starting to question if he cared about me at all.

Emotionally exhausted in the early hours I closed my eyes falling into an unconscious sleepy nightmare. When I woke a few hours later the sun had begun to rise, taking away the shadows of the night that had haunted me. The door to the tent unzipped and Seb stepped in.

'Have you slept? Eaten?' He asked.

I was choked with emotion. 'It was the worst night of my life. I have never ever felt so scared.' I spluttered.

'I can only imagine.'

'I thought that you'd done it on purpose.' I said.

'I know how scared you are of the dark, I remember you telling me about your biggest fear the night we sat around the fire. I'd never purposely do that to you.' He replied, his voice cold.

Despite Seb's reassurance I felt an odd feeling creeping through my veins.

'I need to sleep.' I said.

I lay down and as I closed my eyes I see a hint of a smile on Seb's face. I sleep deeply but with visions of torture and death and a darkness that is more than just lack of light. It is a darkness that seeps into my skin, holding me hostage in my slumber, forbidding me to emerge from the unconscious suffering I am experiencing. When I do wake, I am anxious and edgy and I feel nauseous with the adrenalin that has been coursing through my body for the past twenty-four hours.

'I'm hungry. I had nothing to eat because you had the matches and I couldn't light the camping stove or the fire.' I said as I looked at Seb.

'Shit, I never thought about that. We'll go into the next village, and you can go buy yourself some food, but you'll have to wear a cap and maybe put your hair up.'

We drove until we came to a small village with only a few shops, Seb figured the quieter the area, the less chance of us being spotted.

I walked into the shop and a large friendly woman started chatting away as soon as I entered. I grabbed bread, cereal, milk, two sausage rolls, and some snacks and I placed them on the counter.

'You're new to the area. Where are you staying love?' She threw the question at me catching me off guard. I faltered and then stood there with my mouth open trying to think of what to say.

'Just down the road,' I said avoiding eye contact. I saw her frown.

'Is that Browns Farm?' She beemed. 'They are lovely aren't they, but I'm not sure why you're buying all of this food because Brenda always makes delicious meals.'

'Oh no, not there, just along from there.'

She stopped ringing the food in and looked me in the eye.

'But there *is* nowhere along from there. There's only Browns and then it's a good eight mile to the next house.'

I flushed red and stood awkwardly as she juggled scanning the items and thinking about what I'd just said. She was suspicious I could see it in her eyes. She kept glancing at me and as she took my money.

'I'm sure I've seen your face somewhere before. Are you sure you've not been in this area before?' She asked.

'Oh yes, silly me,' I said, hitting my forehead. 'I came here a few years ago.'

'Did you stay at Browns then?'

What the fuck was with her obsession with the Browns?

'Yeah, yeah, I did.' I handed her the money and took the bag. 'See you and thanks.'

I made for the door as fast as I could, and I could see her following me. I got in the car and looked back as Seb pulled away and she was looking through the glass door.

'You were a while. I almost sent in a search party but then I guessed there will already be one looking for you.' He laughed.

THIRTY-SIX

Laila

It took almost two hours of driving before Seb found a spot that was close enough to a river but also secluded from the road. He put the tent up and I gathered some dry twigs and leaves to get a fire going.

'Fire's lit,' he said, as he stood next to the burning mound of twigs and leaves, smoke obscuring him as it swirled around in the air.

Later that night Seb opened a bottle of whiskey. We sat in camp chairs next to the fire and watched as sparks danced in the night air. Seb was in a good mood now and I felt less anxious.

'I was thinking, mum's had time to think about us, and she knows that we are serious. Maybe I could call her and-.'

'You're taking the piss right?' he asked, and his mood turned as dark as the night sky.

'It was just a thought. It's fine don't worry.' I said quickly. 'I thought, well I didn't think and now that I say it out loud it sounds kind of stupid.' I was waffling.

'Kind of stupid! It *is* fucking stupid! In fact, it's one of the dumbest things to come out of your mouth, and that's saying something. You know for a fact that if we go back I'm in big trouble, or is that your plan? You're bored and now you want your mammy.'

I started to cry, more in anticipation of him leaving in a mood again, but also because no matter how hard I tried I always seemed to get it wrong. He got out of his chair, and I was frantic that he was going to take off again so I ran at him to beg him not to leave. He pushed me and I fell to the ground, I grabbed his ankle, all the while pleading with him not to go, and the last thing I remembered was his foot pulling back in slow motion, making its way towards my face.

I woke to mostly darkness. Out of one eye I could see the flickering glow of fading embers in the fire: wood clinging to heat giving an occasional glow of light before dissipating. My head was throbbing, and I tried to recall what had happened and then panic hit me in the chest. Seb had kicked me. Where was he? I yelled his name countless times as I tried to get to my feet. When I finally found my balance and the world stopped spinning, I realized that he'd done it again, he'd left me on my own; the car was gone. I collapsed onto the ground and curled up into a ball and in the distance, I heard a siren and I contemplated trying to reach the road to flag someone down.

I wake in the ambulance and the paramedic is talking about having a daughter a little younger than me and how relieved my parents will be that I'd been found. He said how nothing was ever that bad that it couldn't be sorted out. I smiled, but the weight of his words crushed me.

I stayed in hospital overnight because it was late when I arrived. I had an MRI to rule out damage to my brain and a scan to check my oesophagus from the strangulation.

I hated not having any form of contact from Seb and I felt so confused by his actions. Maybe he panicked and then took off, afraid that he'd badly hurt me. I had no idea of knowing when I would hear from him again and that hurt. I felt torn in two, part of me craving him like an addiction, the other part desperate to get away from him.

'Your mum and brother are on their way here. I just spoke to her.' One of the nurses said gently, as if I might break if she spoke too loud. Her name badge told that she was Jenny. She smiled at me with a warmth that helped dissipate the anxiety I felt.

A few hours later my mum entered the room and let out a sob. Anguish evident on her face. Tears of happiness and grief flowed as we cried and hugged. For now, her face was full of relief but I was sure that the anger and questioning would come later.

Chadd was talking non-stop, and telling me off for running away, saying how stressed everyone had been. I could see mum trying to shush him, but he just kept going on about how night times were the worst because he would lie in bed and worry about where I was.

I waited on the doctor discharging me and we sat in the room, filling the gaps with meaningless chit-chat as unanswered questions hung in the air between us. My mind was in overdrive as I wondered how could I return to school as if nothing had happened? I had been on the news for god's sake, I was talk of the town and my one and my only friend Alice was most likely barred from hanging out with me now.

I walked into the house and soaked up the familiar sights in front of me, and the first thing I did was walk upstairs and run a bath. I looked in my bedroom, my haven. I lay on my bed and allowed some tears to fall as I contemplated what might happen next. I had no way of knowing whether Seb wanted to see me again, and if he did, I doubted that I would be allowed. The atmosphere felt charged, all of us wanting to ask questions, but too afraid of upsetting one another.

The next day I was eating breakfast and mum was buzzing about the kitchen pretending to clean even though the place was spotless.

'What is it mum, you're walking on eggshells around me.'

She breathed a sigh of relief.

'The police called to say that they have taken out a domestic violence order against Seb, so that means he can't come anywhere near you and if he does all you have to do is call the police and he will be arrested.'

I started to cry because it felt so final.

'You do understand that if he had really loved you, he wouldn't have hurt you, Laila.' She hugged me and then started twisting her wedding rings which was something she did when she was stressed. You're not the first person he has done this to either.' Mum said gently. She then dropped the bombshell that his real name was Aleksander Petrov and she told me that he had planned the whole thing as some form of revenge. I struggled to process what she was saying and the physical pain I felt was unlike anything I had ever experienced.

'It's not true, it can't be!' I cried.

'I'm so sorry darling but it is.' She said as she wiped a tear off her cheek.

'So me and him, it was all fake? All a way of getting back at you for my dad killing his dad?' I was dumbfounded.

Mum nodded.

I lay on my bed for an hour thinking about how I could word a text message to Seb. I just couldn't get my head around our relationship being some kind of cruel joke or revenge against my family. The things that he'd said to me were so real. The times that we'd made love were real and the plans for our future had been real.

I called him, heart beating loudly in my ears as I left a voicemail. *'It's me. I need to talk to you.'* I say before hanging up and letting the tears flow. I cried as I re-lived everything. I visualized him standing outside of the school next to his car, looking handsome and cool. I could see the other girls flirting with him but he'd only looked at me. Why would he choose me out of everyone in the school? But then a memory of us laughing and talking about our future would quash the doubts that strangled me. My phone chimed and I picked it up. It was a text message from him. My heart faltered as I swiped the screen to read it and my worst fears were confirmed.

I guess by now you know the truth. If I was you I would be very careful what you tell the police otherwise things could get pretty uncomfortable for you. I'm sure mummy wouldn't want any videos of her daughter posted online or naked pictures put on social media, and just incase you can't remember what you looked like, I'll jog your memory.

Three attachments followed. The first photo was from the day I first skipped school, when Seb got me drunk. I was lying totally naked on a blanket with the wine bottles next to me. The next was another one of me from when we smoked dope in the wigwam. I was naked from the waist up and the third was one from when he encouraged me to strip-off and wash in the river. I sobbed and sobbed as reality crashed down around me. My mum was right. The whole thing had been a set up from the beginning. Getting me drunk, encouraging me to smoke weed, get naked, it had all been about him gathering evidence against me. I was heartbroken.

Mum came into my room.

'What is it Laila?'

'I hate him.' I yelled as I threw my phone.

Mum consoled me as I cried myself to sleep, and I wished more than anything that I had listened to her because as much as I'd hated what she'd had to say, she had been right about everything.

THIRTY-SEVEN

Dani

I attempted to do meditation to calm my nerves. Today was the day that Laila was going to speak to the police. I felt so nervous for her, and I was worried about her emotional state. I heard her crying often, but whenever I tried to comfort her she would just sob silently and tell me that she was fine.

'Laila are you ready?'

She walked into the room dressed in yesterdays jeans and t-shirt.

'You should have made more effort honey. You could wear your black trousers and a nice top.' She fired me a death stare as if I had suggested attending the police station naked. I said nothing. She was stressed enough.

As we sat in the car and pulled off the drive, I looked at her. My poor girl seemed weighed down.

'How are you feeling honey?' She shrugged but did not reply. 'You make sure you tell the police everything you know. I can't come in with you, you do know that don't you.'

'I want to do this by myself anyway.' She stated firmly.

'Ok darling, I'll be waiting for you in reception.'

Just over an hour later Laila walked out in a rush to leave.

'Can I have a word?' The Sergeant asked.

I hand Laila the car keys and wait until she is out of the door.

'I just wanted to let you know that Laila is backing Mr Petrov's story that she was the one that suggested they abscond. She claims that Mr Petrov treated her well and did not harm her in any way. Of course we know otherwise from Laila's injuries, but unless Laila gives us some evidence, we will not be able to charge him with assault. She is sixteen and can legally leave home if she chooses to. She denies that her attacked her and claims that she tripped and fell against a rock after drinking too much.'

'But that's ridiculous. It's obvious that the whole thing was all planned to get back at me.'

'Unfortunately, theory is not enough. The law states that we need proof and believe me we have tried. Sadly, without evidence we cannot charge him. If Laila changes her mind and wants to make another statement, please bring her in.'

'I guess you see this a lot.' I said, feeling defeated. 'People getting off because they know how to work the system, or they intimidate their victims so that they remain silent.'

'More often than I would like.' She confirmed.

I walked to the car, angered at the thought of that man roaming free after everything he had put us all through. I was under no doubt that he was behind her statement.

'Would you like to go for a coffee or a milkshake?' I asked, as I pulled out of the car park. I was struggling to hold back the barrage of questions that were forcing their way into my mouth. Breathe *Dani. She's been through enough.*

I drove to The Coffee Nook, a café with window seats and alcoves where people could hide away from the world. It had a community library where locals dropped off books they no longer wanted, and customers could help themselves to a new novel while topping up on caffeine. It always smelled of coffee and cinnamon.

We found a seat with a window overlooking parkland, and I ordered drinks.

'Was it harder than you thought it would be honey?' I asked Laila, gently.

'I'd rather not talk about it.' She said, and looked away from me, avoiding eye contact. I paused for a few seconds before responding.

'I know that you told the police that it was all your idea.' She doesn't respond. 'Has he threatened you in some way Laila? Because if he has, I need to know.'

Tears fall out of her eyes like rain falling from a threatening storm, and all I want to do is hug her, but she brushes me off. I try to change the subject to lighten the mood.

'You can go back to school next week,' I said brightly. She looked at me horror stricken, all wide eyed and open mouthed.

'You're joking right? You can't expect me to go back after everything. The whole school will know, all of the teachers will know. I can't. I can't mum!' Laila is hyperventilating, gasping at the air around her as if she was running out of time. Her eyes were wild as her terror built momentum. In a split second she ran out of the café while gasping and sobbing.

Eventually her breathing slowed, but huge sobs escape her every now and then. I had never witnessed Laila have a panic attack before and it was not something I ever wanted to witness again. I held her until her breathing eased.

'Darling what's wrong?' I asked, but my words seemed so futile. I knew what was wrong. She had been through so much and she couldn't face any more. I more than anyone understood how that felt.

'Don't make me go back mum. I can't face them all whispering and asking questions, calling me names.' She starts to work herself up again and I say the first words that come in to my head.

'Shhh, it's fine. You don't have to go back there. Stop crying...' I know as I speak the words that I have promised something that I should not have. I have taken it upon myself to make one of the biggest decisions of my daughter's life in a bid to calm her.

Chadd wasn't happy to hear that Laila was not returning to school. I tried talking to him about her panic attack and how she'd been through a lot but he just didn't get it and started yelling about her getting special treatment and how he would never have been allowed to drop out of school. He experienced one of her panic attacks first hand the following morning. Like the day before, Laila started hyperventilating to the point where we thought she was going to pass out. She was inconsolable and begging for an ambulance in between breathy sobs. Chadd and I were besides ourselves trying to figure out if we let her ride it out or actually call an ambulance.

'Now do you see? It's not pretty is it?' I said to Chadd once Laila had settled enough to be left alone.

'She still needs to finish school, mum.' Chadd said, brow furrowed in concern for his sister.

'I know. I have to find her another school.' I was well aware that moving school may not solve the issue but until Laila had finished her exams we would have to find a way through this.

I felt such shame seeing the worry etched on Chadd's face and I often felt resentment that I had to be both mother and father. There would always be a part of me angry with Luke, even though he set us free.

I walked upstairs and knocked on Laila's bedroom door.

'Come in.'

I opened the door and was hit with a smell of incense.

'Would you like to come for a walk around the lake with me?' I asked.

Laila bit her lip as if faced with a difficult decision. She nodded and put her book down and slid her shoes on.

I was locking the front door when I heard Laila make strange breathing sounds. I looked at her and followed her eyes that were fixed at the bottom of the driveway. When I looked to see what was causing her distress, I saw *him* parked on the opposite side of the road, window down, staring at her while smoking a cigarette. The anger inside of me swelled like a tidal wave and I marched forward towards him.

'Fuck off away from my house before I call the police.' I yelled, shocked at myself.

He laughed, slowly put his window up and then drove away at a snails pace. I turned around and Laila was sobbing. I suddenly understood the saying "an eye for an eye" because the rage I felt for the man that had turned our lives upside down was worse than the hatred and revenge I'd felt towards Pez.

THIRTY-EIGHT

Laila

It had been three months since I had returned home yet in some ways it felt as if it was three days.

The pain was still raw, and I doubted whether I would ever trust a man again. I wondered how many people Seb had shown my photos to, and paranoia became my new best friend as I convinced myself that strangers knew all about the things we had done.

I had texted Seb far more than I should have but I needed answers. My head was ready to explode with the realisation that he wasn't who I thought he was, and this had all been some sort of sick game to get back at my mum. His name was Aleksander, and that name just did not fit him. And then there was the story behind my father's death. The real story, not the one mum fabricated to *protect us.* Mum refused to tell me what was behind it all. She pretended she didn't know, but I could see she was keeping something from me. Every week without fail Seb would send me a picture or video of me naked, drunk, or even in the shower. He had filmed me without me knowing about it and he even had a video of us having sex. I was mortified. I cried myself to sleep most nights and struggled to wake the next day. My body felt too heavy and every movement, an effort. I was so tired, and I couldn't seem to shake myself out of the black pit of despair that I had fallen into. I knew that my mum was worried about me. I had moved school and I played out the motions of life, but I felt empty inside.

That night as I lay in bed my stomach churned and rolled, making me feel sick. My anxiety was worse than it had ever been. I placed my hand on my stomach to try and stop the feeling of nausea that radiated through me. My stomach flipped, butterflies taking flight within me. I drank some chamomile tea to ease my anxiety.

It took me several more weeks of denial and internet exploring to accept that I might be pregnant. My shape had barely changed, my stomach slightly protruded but not in a noticeable way, but my missed periods and stomach flutters were a definite give away. I thought back to when I was living with Seb and I realized that I not had a period for almost five months. I'd been so stressed when I was with him that I'd not really noticed as time ran away with us. When I had returned home, I thought that the stress of what had happened was to blame and then I had forgotten about it.

The following day I took a bus into town after school and walked into a large chemist. I burnt with embarrassment as I handed the money over to the cashier who only looked a year or two older than me, guilt now stamped on my forehead like a temporary tattoo.

I sat in my room and held the unwrapped test in my hand. I was terrified and praying that there was some other explanation for the lack of monthlies. I peed on the stick and waited; heart beating loudly in rhythm to the seconds that I watched tick by.

'Laila I'm home.' Mum yelled up the stairs, and I shoved the pregnancy test under my pillow as I heard Chadd pound up the stairs two at a time.

'Guess what I did today?' Chadd asked, as he burst through my door.

'Can you knock! It's so rude to just come in here.' I yelled.

'Urgh, what's up with you?' he walked out then shouted down to mum that I'm in a mood.

'Laila are you OK?' Mum shouted up the stairs.

'Yes!' I snapped. 'I just wish people would leave me alone.'

'Food will be thirty minutes.' She said, before telling Chadd to leave me be.

I pulled the test out from under the pillow and stared at the window. Pregnant. Oh fuck, fuck, fuck! I felt sick for a different reason now! I tried to think about how I could break the news to my mum, and I couldn't think of the words to say to her. I was stunned and shocked. I was sixteen years old, and I was pregnant to a man that had used me and who had absolutely no feelings for me.

'Dinner's ready!'

I sat at the table and pushed the pasta and chicken around my plate. My mind was still processing the fact that I had a life growing inside of me.

'You're terribly quiet.' Mum said, her voice thick with concern.

'I'm just not hungry, sorry.'

'Make sure you have some cereal before bed if you're not eating dinner.' She fussed.

I nodded and left the table.

'Laila.' I turned. 'You will have to eat your dinner tomorrow; you're not making a habit of this.' She said, quietly but firmly.

I lay on my bed and put my hands on my stomach. I'm just not sure how to feel about being pregnant. Part of me wanted to run away from myself, and the other part wanted to pretend it wasn't happening. I try to visualize myself with a pram and a baby but I can't. I wonder if Seb will want to be involved and then I feel stupid and remind myself he's not even called fucking Seb.

Two weeks later I sit in the doctor's surgery. It's school holidays and there are toddlers and kids running riot. I shudder to myself in disbelief that I could be running after my own screaming child in the near future. I breathe in the smell of disinfectant and I notice a picture of a baby breast-feeding.

The LED message board eventually spells out my name and I swallow the lump that's formed in my throat as I walk past the other patients towards the doctor's room. I enter the room and sit down. Nerves rise up in my throat rendering me speechless.

'Hi Laila.' My name is Dr Karish. How can I help you?' The female doctor asked.

I wring my hands together forcing the words from my mouth.

'I'm pregnant.' I blurt out.

I see the split-second shock before she rights herself and becomes professional again.

'I take it you've done a test at home?' She smiles at me. 'How pregnant do you think you are?'

'I'm not sure.' I said, looking at things on her desk to avoid eye contact.

'Can you remember when your last period was?'

'About five months ago I think.' She raised an eyebrow.

'Can you lie on the couch for me please, I want to have a feel of your stomach and then I will book you in for a scan. Just pull down your skirt slightly and pull your shirt up a little.'

I feel as if my life has taken on a surreal element. I zoned out as the doctor probed and pressed my stomach. I think I hear her sigh, but I'm not sure.

'How do you feel about being pregnant?'

'I'm not sure, I've just found out so...'

'Do your parents know?'

I shake my head and turn to face the wall.

'Do you think they will be supportive?'

'It's just mum, my dad died when I was a baby. I'm not sure about how my mum would feel but I don't think she'll be happy.'

The doctor looked at me sympathetically. 'The thing is Laila, given that you haven't had a period for five months, it may be too late to make any decisions about the baby. I hear the words, but nothing really registers.

'Do you understand what that means?' She paused, and I look at her. 'It means that you will have to go ahead with the pregnancy.'

I say nothing. My brain and body have turned numb, and I am feeling no emotion.

'I think the next thing to do is book you in for a scan. I'll make a call and see if I can speed that up for you.'

She picks up the phone and my head plays out a movie clip of me with a baby in my arms. It feels wrong.

'Laila.' The doctor interrupts. 'I have booked you in for a scan this Thursday at three pm. It might be a good idea to talk to your mum before then.' She said gently. She handed me a note with information for my scan and I leave the room. I feel tears spring to my eyes as reality starts to hit about the situation that I am in. There's no denying it. I am pregnant, I have no future with the father, and I have not even left school yet. My life is over.

I do not go to the scan and the weeks ticked by. My stomach grows slightly but it is small enough to hide it under long t-shirts and jumpers. I live in a strange state of denial; aware but terrified. And when my brain starts mulling over my situation I distract myself to avoid the flood of anxiety it creates.

As I open the door, a smell of cooking hits me like a wall of mist and my stomach somersaults.

'Hi honey. I've made your favourite meal. Chicken and leek pie,' mum beams a smile at me.

'Oh. Cool,' I say, thinking back to when I last declared that as my favourite meal and I reckoned I must have been about seven years old.

'Should be ready in an hour.'

'Can I just have a small portion please mum, I'm not feeling too good.' I see her bite on her lip, the veil of worry drops down and I can tell that she's chewing my words over in her mind.

'Laila, I think we should get you some routine blood tests done at the doctors, you've not been eating properly and...' I zoned out, not wanting to listen to the lecture.

'Yeah, OK,' I replied, too lethargic to debate it with her. I climbed the stairs, my limbs weighed down with blood made of lead, and I lay down on my pillow and closed my eyes. I woke with a pain in my stomach, and I rushed to the toilet. I must have picked up the virus from school.

I tried to eat dinner but was more focused on the internal pains shooting through me before I needed to make a mad dash to the toilet.

'Mum, can I heat this up later or eat it tomorrow please? I don't feel well.'

'Try and eat something please Laila.'

'Yeah, try and eat some more, Laila.' Chadd echoed, and I glared at him. I pushed my chair back from the table so that I could escape them both and I hear mum sigh. I take a shower and lie on my bed, groaning with the pains wondering if I might have food poisoning. I wrap myself up under the duvet and try to sleep for a few hours. I am woken with pains shooting through me like electric shocks. I hear mum go to bed and the landing light go off and a little while later a pain rips me apart and I shout involuntarily, unable to stop the sounds that escape my mouth. The pain gets stronger and stronger and I suddenly feel terrified of my own body.

I hear mum open her door and see a light filter through into my room.,

'Laila what is it? I can hear you in my room.' She makes towards me and touches my brow. 'You're sweating honey'.

I wriggle as another pain radiates from within and turns me into some sort of animal that omits inhumane noise. I scream. Mum stares at me, ashen white.

'Chadd, call an ambulance I think it's her appendix.' Chadd who had just walked in the doorway rushed out of the room.

'Come on honey you need to try and stand up so ...' She freezes as another scream erupts from my mouth and simultaneously, my vagina feels as if it has been set on fire. I push with a force that comes from outside of me, a primeval energy that takes over my whole being, and eventually I feel the pain subside and I relax a little, taking in big gulps of air before it starts over again. Mum is panicking and crying, yelling out to Chadd to ask how long the ambulance will be. Time freezes as a muffled sound fills the silence. Mum pulls the bed sheets from me and takes three steps backwards, banging her head on my wardrobe. She stays there staring for what feels like minutes but it's only seconds. She rushes forward suddenly and I cower, momentarily frightened by her movement. She keeps opening her mouth but it's like her volume level is on mute.

I close my eyes and mum starts yelling for Chadd and then she lifts a baby off the bed while sobbing loudly. The baby hangs there, like a doll, moving only when mum gently hits it. It's waxy and bluish in colour. I lie dumbfounded as I watch my mother, eyes wide with disbelieve and alarm. My brother walks in just as the baby let's out a piercing scream and mum sinks onto my bed and breaks down. Chadd mutters *what the fuck* before he backs out of the room. Mum stares at me, stupefied.

'You've had a baby. A daughter.' She says, her voice hoarse. Her face pale with shock.

I looked at her but said nothing, my brain was still catching up and processing the fact that I was now a mother myself. A siren breaks the stillness and mum looked at me, and then at the baby that she had wrapped in a towel and was now reluctantly cradling.

The next hour is chaotic with paramedics checking me and the baby over, while mum put some clothing into a bag, muttering about having nothing for a baby in this house. Once at hospital I was placed in a room with two other mothers who were much older than me. They are both married. I know this because they make a point of telling me. They glance at me and then at each other, and a silent conversation takes place between their disproving eyes.

I pull the curtain to block the prying eyes. I feel slightly deranged. Even though I knew this was going to happen, a part of me had hoped it wouldn't.

'Now then what's going on here?' A nurse asked as she whipped the curtain back. 'We can't have you shutting yourself away. You need to feed your daughter so I will show you how.'

I waited for her to get a bottle out and she stood, looking at me expectantly. 'You need to BREAST feed your daughter.' She emphasized the word breast as if speaking to a child.

'Oh no, I'm bottle feeding.' I mumbled, red faced.

'Nonsense. Breast is best. You haven't even tried.'

'No honestly it's fine.' I said quietly, avoiding eye contact. She had eyes that could bore a hole in the ground.

'Formula costs money you know.' She said, accusingly. I stayed silent and eventually she marched off and returned with a bottle.

Sweat formed on my top lip as I eased the baby out of her crib and settled her in the crook of my arm. I could feel eyes burning into me as the other two mothers watched my every move. I pushed the teat into her mouth and watched her suckle the milk from the bottle as if her life depended upon; and it hit me, that it did. I looked at her tiny finger nails and the whisp of hair that was still matted with remnants of blood. She was dressed in a baby-grow that was too big for her, but she was perfect.

I shook with nerves as I sat her upright and tried to wind her, frightened that I might hurt her in some way.

'Hold her head forward like this,' the blonde woman to my left said. 'Pat or rub her on the back, you can be a little firmer to help her bring her wind up.' I smiled and thanked her. I looked at the other woman, but she turned away from me and focused on her little boy who she kept calling Thomas Tittlemouse.

A little while later mum walked in with a bag that was brimming with clothes and nappies. I only got a few items until we know what's happening ...'

I digested her words and gave them back to her. 'Until we know what's happening? What does that mean mum?' I asked her.

'I'd rather not have the discussion here in front of strangers, but you know – if you decide that you're keeping the baby. This is a huge responsibility, Laila. You're just a child yourself and you haven't even left school yet. We have no baby items at home. For God's sake we don't even have a baby seat to take her home in. Do you know how much baby things cost? And how do you plan to look after her when you are still at school and have no money?'

'Well I'm pleased that you held back from having the discussion you didn't want to have in front of strangers.' She flushed red and glanced behind her. I can't just give her away. Look at her!'

Mum stands up and pulls the curtain around us.

'Laila it's not that I don't want you to keep her, but I'm still adjusting to the shock of this baby. Why didn't you tell me that you were pregnant?'

'I was scared, and I hoped it would go away.' I said, as tears fell.

'I guess that's all irrelevant now. Are you saying you want to keep her?' Mum's eyes fell on the crib and her face softened.

'Yes, but I will need help.'

'And this is the part that worries me. We still have a lot to talk about.'

'Well other people mange, so I will. Somehow.'

'It might take your brother a little longer to come around. He's barely spoke a word since yesterday. And I have yet to break the news to your gran.'

I felt shame envelop me, but I was aware that there was nothing I could say to change the reality of my situation.

I watched mum leave and tears welled up in my eyes as the void between us lay visible for all to see.

Three days later the doctor allowed us to go home. The baby had spent some time under the UV light because she had a touch of jaundice but she was doing well now.

I was waiting on my mum arriving with a car seat when gran walked into the room. I froze, unsure what to say to her. Gran smiled and I mirrored her, smiling back.

'How are you? How's the baby?' She looked in the transparent plastic crib and a smile spread across her face, which was quickly swallowed up by a look of sadness that fell like a shadow.

'She's good.' I said awkwardly. It felt weird and I wasn't sure how to be around her anymore.

'I won't lie Laila, I am devastated that you have had a baby at such a young age. Your mum and I have always hoped that you would travel the world and live life before you had the responsibility of being a parent.'

'I will still be able to do that gran, just a little later.' I said nervously.

'It's not that easy my love. Once you have a child the responsibility is always there.'

'But she is here *now*, and I can't turn back the clock.'

She nodded. 'Have you thought of a name yet?'

'Evie. I am calling her Evie.'

Gran gingerly picked her out of the cot.

'Hello there Evie' she said.

A tear trickled down my face and I smiled for the first time in weeks.

The first four months at home with Evie were a nightmare. I was exhausted and being catapulted into motherhood overnight was such a shock to my system. There was no more 'me' time.

I had a nightly bath in peace and that was it. Evie slept in my room with me and I attempted to fit school work in around her, which left me in tears on many an occasion. However, she really was a little ray of sunshine, and despite mum's initial shock, she adored Evie. Months passed by, along with Evie's first Christmas, and I won't say that things were easy, but we managed to find a routine that worked for us: most of the time.

THIRTY-NINE

Dani

It was two days before Evie's first birthday, and I watched her bash pieces of banana on the tray of her highchair before shovelling them into her mouth. She gave me a smile that revealed her four teeth.

'Who's going to have a birthday soon?' I sang, and Evie clapped and smiled even though she has no clue what I was talking about.

'Let's bake cupcakes for your party tomorrow.' Laila said, and Evie gurgled a response.

Laila was elbow deep in flour when there was a tap at the door. I saved my work and when I opened the door there was a present on the doorstep. A box wrapped in pink ballet shoe paper. I opened the matching gift tag. *Have a great birthday, Evie. See you soon.* I figured Mrs Grant from next door must have left it.

I brought it in and placed it on the dining table next to the party paraphernalia.

'Laila I'm just going to the shops. Do I need to get anything aside from Evie's cake?'

'No, mum, everything's sorted.'

I parked my car and walked towards the shop to pick up Evie's birthday cake. There are flower beds packed with clusters of pansies and a low thrum of bees doing their work as they dart from flower to flower. A bell rings as I enter the shop and nostalgia hits me as I inhale the smell of boiled sweets, chocolate, and marzipan.

Display cabinets house trays of delicate looking chocolates and shelves hold jars with homemade toffees, and sweets. It reminds me of my childhood when Elanor would cook up batches of cinder toffee, lemon twists, and marzipan balls dipped in chocolate. I peek inside the box to approve Evie's cake and can't help but smile.

'This is amazing. Thank you again.' I hand my card over to pay and smile at the young girl who is probably not much older than Laila.

Outside, the smell of spring is in the air and people look less weighed down. I think about Laila and even though deep in my heart there was an ache of sadness that her life had turned out this way, I was also incredibly proud of her. She had stepped up as a mother and cared for Evie from the get-go. Her life had changed overnight but she had rarely complained, even though I saw the tiredness on her face and sensed that she was grieving for the freedom she had taken for granted. She had managed to pass her exams, not the results she had originally been predicted, but enough to get her into college when Evie was a little older. She had even requested books about nursing and midwifery for her birthday, which showed how dedicated she was. My baby girl was now a young woman, a determined, strong young woman.

I was making my walking back to my car when I heard a whistle; not a wolf whistle, more a trying to get someone's attention whistle. I ignored it and kept walking, and then a car horn beeped, making me jump. I looked to my right and the window of the blue Vauxhall slowly dropped and Seb – Aleksander was staring back at me with a wide grin on his face.

'Long time no see, Dani.' I dropped the cake and let out a cry. I wasn't sure if I was distraught over the cake or horrified at seeing his face. I stood frozen on the spot, and he pressed a button on his steering wheel and Florence and the Machine blasted out through the window as he mouthed the lyrics:

Holy water cannot help you now. A thousand armies couldn't keep me out. I don't want your money I don't want your crown. See I have to burn your kingdom down.

I was rooted to the spot. The song ended and he stared at me. 'This couldn't have worked out any better really Dani. Just think, it was almost eighteen years ago when you took my father from me.' He paused. Letters rolled around my mouth like jelly, slithering away before I had a chance to form them into words.

'Now look at us!' He shouts, making me jump. His eyes dance and his mouth twitches. He is mocking me.

'Now – now I have given you the best revenge present in the form of your granddaughter. My little Evie: and every time you look at her, you will be reminded of me.'

With that he sped off and I let his words sit on my tongue, thawing like ice, and I cried. I cried because no matter how hard I tried I could not seem to outrun my past.

FORTY

Further Reading

Other books by the author:

With This Ring – 2016

When Charlotte Jackson first sets eyes on Joe Porter, she falls in love with him almost instantly. He is attractive, charming and everything she could dream of in a boyfriend.Joe's love and protection for Charlotte spiral out of control as their relationship intensifies, until Charlotte finds herself isolated and a victim of domestic violence.After a series of horrifying events, Charlotte flees the country and heads to Australia to live with her family and start her life over. She excels at her career and over time learns to heal the wounds of her former life.One day, out of the blue, a ghost from the past revisits her and makes her question everything all over again.

What unfolds will change her life forever. But will it be for better or for worse?

Tick Tock – 2018

Dani is young, beautiful, sexy and impulsive. Born into a wealthy family, she has never wanted for anything; but the death of her father at an early age has left her yearning for love and affection. When Luke and Dani meet, she falls hard for him, but her naivety and impulsiveness finds her drawn into the world of crime. Luke takes matters into his own hands and tracks Dani down overseas in a bid to retrieve the money she owes. A twist in the plan results in Dani paying the ultimate price for her actions. Dani finds herself held hostage, and forced to become part of a world she never knew existed in order to pay her 'debt' back. The clock is ticking ...

Dancing with Dragonflies – 2023

What would you do if the person most precious to you was taken from you?

Mel had everything she had ever wanted. She married the love of her life; they built the house of their dreams, and they brought a daughter into the world. What she never envisaged was that three would become two.

After the death of their child, Mel struggles with the devastating loss. Her journey through grief will take her on solo adventures and see her cross paths with people who both challenge and inspire her.

Will she find the love that she deserves? Will she forgive herself enough to move forward, or will she remain stuck in the past?

Printed in Great Britain
by Amazon

28263675R00116